TUG of WAR

CATHERINE FORDE

[signature] 4/9/07

EGMONT

EGMONT

We bring stories to life

First published in Great Britain 2007
by Egmont UK Limited
239 Kensington High Street
London W8 6SA

Text copyright © 2007 Catherine Forde
Cover copyright © 2007 Marina Caruso

The moral rights of the author and cover illustrator have been asserted

ISBN 978 1 4052 2005 7

1 3 5 7 9 10 8 6 4 2

www.egmont.co.uk
www.catherineforde.co.uk

A CIP catalogue record for this title is available from the British Library

Typeset by Avon DataSet Ltd, Bidford on Avon, Warwickshire
Printed and bound in Great Britain by the CPI Group

In memory of my Granny Mochan

Thank you to the following peachy brilliant title consultants of St Aloysius' College, Glasgow: Ciadhra McGuire, Amy Johnstone, Katie McNally, Olivia Dunn, Caitlin McCormick, Jay Chitnis, Clare Burns, David Carnan, Craig Maclean . . . not forgetting Ellen Hughes (As if!).

EGMONT PRESS: ETHICAL PUBLISHING

Egmont Press is about turning writers into successful authors and children into passionate readers – producing books that enrich and entertain. As a responsible children's publisher, we go even further, considering the world in which our consumers are growing up.

Safety First
Naturally, all of our books meet legal safety requirements. But we go further than this; every book with play value is tested to the highest standards – if it fails, it's back to the drawing-board.

Made Fairly
We are working to ensure that the workers involved in our supply chain – the people who make our books – are treated with fairness and respect.

Responsible Forestry
We are committed to ensuring all our papers come from environmentally and socially responsible forest sources.

For more information, please visit our website at
www.egmont.co.uk/ethicalpublishing

CONTENTS

1

Picture This . . .

Look at Mum. She's so funny, squatting above the lid of my suitcase. Her old house-skirt is pulled tight round her thighs. It's the dire one my best pal Adele decided makes Mum's bum look like kittens fighting in a sack. Anyway, I'm kneeling on the suitcase too. All my weight pushing it down. Willing it *shuuuut*.

'Quick, Denis, lock it *now*,' Mum tells my Dad. When she says *now* she drops her big bum –

CRUMP!

– timing it exactly to the sound of another wayyyy-too-close-for-comfort explosion outside.

I catch my Dad wincing. Despite him kidding on he's heard zilch. Shouting 'Bingo!' to cover up whatever's happening to Glasgow tonight as his thumbs nip the sneck of my case.

He sits back on his heels. Wipes his sleeve across his forehead.

'What a palaver,' Mum sighs, floopy-whooshing her hand in front of her face. Her cheeks are red and shiny. I mean redder and shinier than normal. And she's breathless, but she can't help laughing.

When she laughs, I laugh. Can't help myself.

'But who says bits of me aren't handy?' Mum skelps one palm off the side of her bum, the thwack of it *ting-ing-ing-ing* perfectly in time with another crump from the sky. Massive this time. Nearer. As it fades, Mum slumps against my Dad. He puts his arms round her.

From John's room through the wall I hear music being turned up. John's meant to be packing too. Instead he crashes in on his drums over a woman singing. Her voice is bitter-sweet. I know the song. Blondie: 'Picture This'. Really, *really* old . . . It's one of Mum's favourites from her punky days when she swears she was spiky and thin.

Mum shuts her eyes, her head tilting towards John's room as she whisper-sings along to the verse about wanting a photo to carry in her wallet.

Then she stops. Twists round so she can look my Dad in the face.

'Denis, imagine no drumming after tonight. How can we be sending Molly and John away to strangers like this?'

In the candlelight of our hall Mum's eyes have turned glisteny as diamond teardrops.

'Shouldn't they just stay?' she asks my Dad. 'We've all been fine up till now –'

'Kitty, these strikes come thick and fast. We know they're getting worse –'

My Dad circles his hand through the space above us all, then brings it to rest on my hair. 'And you know John's position –'

My Dad's sigh reaches right down to his slippers. His hands cup Mum's face as she nods and shakes her head at the same time.

'But even to put my kids on a *train* these days. Wave them off God knows where. To what? To who? Not knowing when we'll see . . .'

Mum's sigh is deep and massive. Her hands are

pressed to her chest. This means – as John would say – she's Not Calm.

Please, please don't be sad, I will Mum, biting my lip, shutting my eyes tight to stop myself seeing her face crumple.

See, if Mum cries I bet I'll cry too. Then she'll cry more and I'll be so . . . Well, let's face it, is there anything worse than watching your mum break her heart? Right now even the *thought* of Mum crying cramps and spins my tummy so I clutch it. Gasp loud enough for my Dad to lean over Mum. Whisper, 'Shh, Kitty, keep it together for Molly's sake.'

I open my eyes to see my Dad tilt up Mum's face . . .

And *sssshloop* he kisses her for as long as the curfew siren wails anyone off of the streets. And – er – I'm not talking a *pw* on the cheek here. My Dad kisses Mum like they're movie lovers even though he's *fifty-nine* and she's *fifty-eight*. See if I sent Adele a vid-text of *this*:

Check the 2 old snoggers. Can u c tongues!?!? Mollyxxx

Swear. She would just DIE OFF –

Pure Antiques Roadshow *material, older than my granny, let's face facts, Molly,* Adele'd be reminding me.

'Cept you can't text any more. Since The Emergency, every mobile network on the planet's been . . . well, I'm not sure. John says the technical term is *!*!ed. *!*!ed like our landlines and gas and electricity and chances of not being tox-bombed. Which is why, last month, Adele's mum's new Canadian man evacuated my totally best friend and her mum out of Glasgow to Toronto, before things get any worse.

And it's why, first thing tomorrow, I'm leaving too. With John. We're evacuating ourselves before some City Child-Safe programme the Scottish Parliament's set up kicks in for real in Glasgow and Edinburgh and Aberdeen and Dundee and we're Sent Away. John to ForcesUK because he's old enough for the Draft. Me into some camp like I'm an Illegal. On me own. On a train. Miles from Mum. And my Dad. Till The Emergency's over. Probably wearing a stupid big label round my neck like all those miserable Evacuees from World War Two in those ancient films we watched in

5

school. Separated from my family for months.

No ta.

This is bad enough. Me and John going off tomorrow to somewhere my Dad's found. 'And God knows who'll be mothering Molly –' Mum's anxiety gasps out as soon as my Dad takes his lips from hers. Before she can go on he kisses her quiet again.

2
Meet John Now

'But, don't worry, Molly. You'll be home before you know you're away,' my Dad promised me.

This was last week when he called me and Mum into the sitting room. Then he called John. Three times before he appeared.

John swore under his breath when my Dad told us he'd found somewhere *decent* we could stay till things calmed for cities targeted by The Emergency.

''Member Jim Pearson? Accounts, Kitty? You've worked with him,' my Dad began. 'Anyway, his cousin runs a dairy farm that's a B&B. The Emergency's been keeping folk from booking in so his wife fancies taking in a city girl Molly's age to lodge –'

'A farm?' Mum cut in, doing what Adele calls my Mum's spammy-mammy routine and fanning one hand against her chest very fast while whooshing air out her mouth like she's deflating. Means Mum's Not Too Happy.

Neither was John.

'A farm. Yippee!' His mouth curled like he'd just stepped in cowcrap.

'A farm!' I whooped. 'Where?'

'Borders. Beautiful part of Scotland, too.' My Dad smiled at Mum, not me, as he spoke. He sounded worn and saggy.

'It's near Galashiels, so we're handy for the new rail link, Kitty. Means visits up and down if it's safe. Anyway,' my Dad tried to make his voice two stone lighter like Mum wishes she was, 'news keeps saying this carry-on'll be over by Christmas, so with us both out working we'll hardly miss the kids away. Mean-time,' my Dad winked at me like he was announcing Particularly Good News, 'Molly can get back to school. Pearson fella's wife teaches in the local primary . . .'

'No chance. I'm not *at* Primary any more –'

'You're not at any school.' My Dad's hand blocked my winge: STOP. He was already turning to John.

'I've sorted you labouring on a farm near Pearson's. You'll have official papers so you can't get drafted while you're working. Food and lodging in exchange –'

'Hang on, Denis. You mean John won't live with Molly –' Mum didn't even get a chance to fret when John leapt to his feet and bawled so loud you'd think he was holding an invisible mike in his clenched fist.

'Labouring? Forget that. I start yooni in two weeks. I'm nearly eighteen –' John cranked up the volume. Nothing unusual there. All my Dad needs to do is *breathe* and John blows a gasket.

Mind you, his reaction to *this* news was more extreme than normal. Here's the gist, minus all the *!*! words.

Was my Dad INSANE? Treating John like a wean when he was legally adult? None of John's mates had been forced to evacuate Glasgow by their stupid old parents. Why? The hell? Should he?!?!?!!

'Finished, son?'

Funny. See, when my Dad *finally* got a quiet word in, he shut John's pus BIGTIME!

9

'None of your pals left Glasgow. Good for them. Two blown to pieces waiting for a subway. Three called up to serve the king because they're legally adults without jobs. And if you bothered reading the paper I bring in every day you'd learn being a student's not going to protect you now the government needs cannon fodder. I've found you work so your studies can keep, and so might your life. You'll be leaving with your sister in the morning. End of story.'

3
The Beginning

But it's not the end. And this morning's the beginning.

Mind you, Mum's in even more of a state than she was last night.

She has me out my bed at the crack of dawn, helping her find *more* stupid things to pack in my suitcase. Out come half my clothes – the pulse ones, of course – in go baked beans, tins of soup, firelighters, boxes of matches . . .

'Molly won't need this stuff, Kitty,' my Dad tries to convince Mum when he sees what she's doing.

'And all *this* is out of date anyway,' I grumble while Mum makes me hold a candle over the bathroom cabinet. She's sweeping all the old sticky-gicky medicine and pills no one ever uses into a plastic bag.

'Who knows what's ahead, Molly? You might be

thanking me for *these*.' Mum pops two diarrhoea pills into her mouth. 'Just to be on the safe side with my tummy this morning,' she says, 'and better take paracetamol. Oh dear. Best before November 2012. Months out of date. Is that bad? Och, take it anyway. You never know what'll run out next . . .'

While Mum yatters, I flick on and off the dead light switch with the end of my candle. I tap my foot and hum same as John does to wind up my Dad whenever he needs a hand with something and John can't be bothered lending his. And even though I don't want to, even though I know Mum's only footering because she loves me, I answer her back. Not aloud. But with this snide voice that pops into my head and won't go away. It says things while I watch Mum pack. Unpack. Repack. Nasty things.

Look at you fussing, the snide voice wheedles. *Listen to yourself: Take this. Do that. Just to be on the safe side.*

'Just to be on the safe side.'

That's Mum's excuse for cramming my bulging suitcase with all the precious flattened toilet rolls she's been stockpiling for the day the shops really run out.

And for piling *more* sterile water into the back-pack John'll have to carry on the train. He's gonna love that!

For checkingcheckingchecking our tox-tester batteries.

'Molly and John won't even *need* them outside Glasgow,' my Dad promises. Only the big cities get gassed. But Mum insists: *'Just to be on the safe side . . .'*

Of what? We're not even leaving *Scotland*.

In fact, not leaving *Glasgow* at this rate.

Though *I'm* all set, like my Dad warned me to be last night. At the front door. With my suitcase. Even wearing the ear-flap fleece hat John says makes me spong. This is so Mum won't have to nag me to put it on.

Our first train leaves Glasgow for Edinburgh in less than an hour. Mum's taken the morning off work to chaperone us on it.

But where is she? Locked in the toilet.

'Denis,' she's bubbling through the keyhole, 'I can't go through with this.'

My Dad – who's late for work by now – just about manages to keep his patience.

'Kitty, this move'll be good for Molly. No Curfew in the country. She'll be outside playing again. Fresh milk. Clean water . . .'

Through the keyhole my Dad reminds Mum about the generator on the farm. That means permanent electricity. Lights that switch on and stay on. Showers. Hot baths. *The Simpsons* and all those vintage comedies I'm pining for: *Friends*, *Dad's Army*, *Little Britain*, *Scrubs* . . .

Honestly, I'm tempted to push him away from the door to shout, 'What we waiting for Mum? *Arriba!!*'

I don't get John either.

Instead of packing last night he took to droning, 'What about my studies?' Then, and this is completely out of character believe me, he sorted his desk and his bookshelf like he'd morphed into a swot worse than sweaty Cynthia McManus whose dad and big sister were toxed in the subway in one of the first nerve-gas attacks of The Emergency, so I'd to feel sorry for her even though Adele 'n' me think

14

her BO's *worse* than nerve gas . . .

John even dusted down my Dad's printer. Hooked it up to his computer. Sad. Does he think *wanting* it to boot up's gonna shock the national grid back into action after it's been down a year? Unscramble the Web? Google the Internet back to life?

Now, when we're heading for the station, John won't get up. My Dad's trying to wheech the duvet off him without either of them losing the heid.

'Please, son. Don't make things harder. You know you can't stay here.' And my Dad's right.

I mean, even if John doesn't get drafted into ForcesUK, where we live in Glasgow right now's slap bang in the Red Zone (or Good As Dead Zone as Adele's mum's new Canadian boyfriend called our neighbour-hood). Our tenement block overlooks the River Clyde where six new warships are being built. Every one of them is three times beastier than HMS *Daring* which my Dad told me was the biggest warship *ever* built in Scotland when my Dad took me to its launch on the Clyde in 2006. See, the yard's where my Dad works. Mum, too, though she's only part-time, in Personnel.

Imagine knowing both you parents work somewhere *totally* dangerous? It freaks me sometimes, despite Mum swearing the shipyard's special bomb-proof bunkers make her workplace safer than our flat in Laurel Street . . .

Mind you, you can't go *anywhere* safely in Glasgow any more.

STAY HOME! STAY IN! STAY SAFE! posters on every lamp post warn you.

Now we're actually going SOMEWHERE.

Say you'd the choice of living on a farm, or staying in an Enemy Target city where

your water supply's poisoned

and supermarkets don't sell food

and planes you can't hear drop remote bombs

and friends stop coming to school

and you can't phone to check if anyone's OK

or go on MSN or BEBO any more . . .

Here's a tricky question: What would you plump for?

'All set, pet?'

My Dad's closing John's door. There's a helluva

thumping going on behind it.

But at least John's up. My Dad looks grim, despite his fingers gentle in my hair. 'Kitty, I can't be late,' he taps quietly on the bathroom door. His voice sounds squeezed in his throat.

'Go. I'll see you later,' Mum's voice cuts in. Gulpy.

My Dad stares at the bathroom door like he wants to *melt* it. He looks knacked out before his day's even started. Briefcase in one hand, the other rubbing his face. His tox-mask's in that one, boi-oi-oi-nging on its elastic like it wants a bit of attention as well as Mum who's sniffing and snuffling like someone mysteriously swiped all the toilet paper out the bathroom and put it in my suitcase instead of shoes . . .

Dad gives the bathroom one last stare, shouting in a cracked voice, 'Look after yourself, John. I love you, son.' Then he crushes me half to death. Leaves my face stinging from the scratch of his beardie . . .

'Missing you already,' I chime after my Dad, same as I kid him every day.

But everything feels wrong. Like in a bad dream. My Dad's belting along our landing too fast and the words I always sing-song after him are burning my throat. I'm swallowing so I don't scream and upset everyone even more:

Dad, what if I don't see you again?

4
Roll Up! Roll Up!

When me and John finally belt into Queen Street
Station with Mum, I'm surprised there aren't hurdy-
gurdy tunes blasting out the loudspeakers:

CHEER UP GLASGOW!
STUFF THE EMERGENCY!

Honestly. You should see the state of us tumbling
and tripping and getting in everyone's way. The
station's mobbed, full of other people doing what we're
doing and evacuating themselves out of Glasgow
before they're told where to go. There are grannies in
bumfly coats next to their compact cases. Mums, and
even some dads, with just about everything including
the kitchen sink piled round them, while their kids ride

19

all the luggage trolleys up and down the platforms over people's feet. You can practically see wee clouds of stress puffing out of every grown-up's ears. And then suddenly in the middle of everything it's:

TaRa! Here Come the Fogartys!

We're sadder than the tatty clown act me 'n' Adele shouted 'DIRE' at as we walked out of the circus we didn't even want to go to last Christmas, but had to because Adele's mum's new Canadian boyfriend bought us front-row seats to impress Adele's mum . . .

So Roll up! Roll up!

See us Fogartys all shouting at once, giving ourselves a showing up:

'Quick.'

'Mu-um.'

'Wait for me. I can't run on these legs.'

Our racket turns heads. I'm wheeling two cases, both with wonkity wheels. Because Mum suggested I *wear* all four jackets I own (denim, school, rain, puffa) to leave more room in my luggage for tins and toilet rolls, I can't work my arms normally.

Means I've to drag my stupid cases sideyways and

they keep falling over. I'm still wearing my ear-flap hat. Plus a tox-mask perched on top, so my hair's lanked with sweat to my skull. Oh, and I've a pair of spotty pink-and-yellow wellies dangling from my neck.

Mum insisted on buying them. Said I wouldn't be turning my nose up when I'm splashing in farm mud.

The string tying the boots together has rubbed my skin raw, but can I bend my elbows to shift it?

All I can do is moan, 'Mu-um,' and try not to bash John. He'd batter me. He's yanking the suitcase Mum shut with her bum, and it's wonkier and beastier than my two put together. Plus he's shouldering a *massive* holdall full of tinned food.

'This weighs a *!*!ing ton,' *he's* growling in a voice that makes people swerve. You can understand why. He's wearing his mouldy army surplus coat under a parka and he left the house without cleaning his teeth.

Then there's Mum.

'Oh, Oh, Oh. I'm too old and fat and slow for all this rushing,' she's been chanting since we left for the station.

Don't ask me why, but she has at least half a dozen plastic bags looped round her arms. A Boots' bag snags on a man's umbrella as soon as we get in to the station and rips. Are there boots in it?

No.

Just several pairs of flowery pants.

None of them new.

All of them mine.

I just have to kid I don't see them even though this means I'll be heading for the Borders knickerless. If Mum knew *that* right now she'd need oxygen. She's stressed enough.

We're late and the noticeboards are blank, of course, thanks to Homeland Security. We quiz four different station staff for info and they all look us up and down like we're Illegals With Suspicious Devices In Our Luggage. Two of them demand Mum and John's Identicards before we're finally directed to the furthest away platform.

'*That's* the Edinburgh train, folks. See, where the guard's blowing the whistle . . .'

Despite all the stramash John made about leaving Glasgow, he's the one who screams 'Wait up!', then tries to vault the ticket barrier on to the platform. Must've been having a think to himself about my Dad's reasons for sending him away, coz normally he's as active as a mug of Horlicks. Mind you, bent double, thanks to his rucksack of water his athletics look pathetic. Which probably explains why the whistling guard makes some ninja sign with his arms that stops our train.

'C'mon girls!' he shooes me and Mum into a carriage.

The whistle shrieks and we're on our way.

Tothefarmtothefarmtothefarm . . .

5

Never a Dull Moment

We're half way to Edinburgh before Mum finds spare breath to pant, '*Ohhh, in the name of the wee man.*' The train's heaving, and no one's giving up their seat, so she has to flump against the wall between two compartments, shifting her weight from one bad leg to the other.

The half a dozen plastic bags dangling off her wrists are biting into her skin, forcing all the blood to her hands so they bulge purple. I know by the way her chest's heaving she needs her inhaler but when I ask her what pocket it's in she just shakes her head. *Mum, you're a state*, my snide head-voice tuts when I notice how the sweat dribbling down her temples drips on to her blouse, staining it. *Yuk!* John's more worried about the bags Mum's holding.

'Sure they're *all* yours?'

'Definitely.' Mum stares hard into John's eyes so he knows she means it.

'Better be ours, y'know,' he grunts, leaning his forehead on the train window.

'Thinking about Keith,' Mum mouths to me, her face the colour of raw pastry.

'But that bomb was in a briefcase, not a Tesco's carrier . . .' I start to blurt when Mum clamps her hand to her mouth. Of course I think she's trying to shut me up.

'. . . happened in London anyway,' I carry on. Till Mum *really* shuts me up.

'Oh, all this carry on today. I'm awful queasy. Any water?' she tugs at John till he opens his backpack. I see Mum reading Keith's name inked next to John's on the inside flap:

FOGARTY and GRAY. HEEEEEEYYYY!

Now I don't know for sure if it's the sight of that, or the memory of what happened to Keith on a train six months ago on his way to an interview for music college (if I say what you might have nightmares like I did for weeks, so I won't), or maybe it's just hitting Mum that she's going to have to put me and John on a train on our own then wave us off in less than an hour . . .

Anyway, suddenly Mum lets out this gurgly wail that makes everyone on the train gasp and stare at her. Then her legs give way. Before I can dodge, I'm flat on my back on the carriage floor and she's on top of me.

Hey! Isn't it just as well she made me wear four jackets at once after all? Otherwise I'd be putting up with broken ribs and punctured lungs over and above the loss of oxygen I suffer while Mum's dead weight crushes my lungs smaller than peanuts.

Then Mum splutters in my ear and starts wriggling about on her stomach. Her arms and legs are flapping like she's some beached she-whale.

John has to get three men to help before he can heave Mum off me.

'Oh, don't know what happened to me there. The train's that hot and shoogly . . .' Mum tries to explain herself, but I notice no one meets her eye.

'Steamin',' someone mutters up the carriage.

'Or not the full shilling,' says someone else. 'It's her kids I feel sorry for. They're like tinkers.'

'Never a dull moment with us Fogartys, is there?' John mutters grimly once he's settled Mum on the Seat For The Elderly And Infirm in place of the young guy in a suit who swore when John asked if he'd mind moving for a sick lady.

John stays outside the compartment Mum's in, head leaning on the train window, eyes closed, clearly not in a chatting mood.

So I doubt there'd be much point in asking him any of the questions I keep asking myself as our journey carries us further and further from home:

What kind of place are we going to?

How are we going to manage without Mum?

My Dad?

From where I'm standing I can see my Mum's profile. She's staring into middle distance, frowning like she's watching something she doesn't like. One of her hands grips a bottle of water so tight I can see the white bones of her knuckles. The other trembles just above her chest. *My* chest tightens the longer I look at Mum, and my breathing turns all jerky, so I force myself to turn away and actually concentrate for a change on the **KEEP ALERT! KEEP ALIVE!** film that's blaring from the drop-down screens throughout the train. Even though I know it off by heart. When there was power, we'd to watch it daily in school. When there was school. And at home it aired between every telly programme. When we'd telly.

Now it links every song on the radio, and tanks trundle up and down streets with that ancient posh Patsy woman from Mum's ancient *Ab-Fab* DVDs gushing on about not panicking if you smell marzipan.

. . . but mawzipan means nerve gas so put yoa masks on and wolk – neva, neva run – to the nearest safe bunker. Wea yoa mask until the awl clea sownds and breeeathe nowmallee, posh Patsy sighs like she's discussing face cream. Whenever we heard this tape in school me 'n' Adele would mimic posh Patsy's voice and fall about laughing.

Remembah, yoa mahsk filtas mowst toxic substancezzz.

I mean, you only *half* pay attention to a warning like that, same as you *half* know where your nearest fire exit is or what to do if a perv offers you sweeties. Who wants to deal with *that* kinda stuff?

I don't.

Unless something Really Not Calm's happening.

E.g. your mum looking more sad and scared and worried than you've ever seen her.

I watch the film right through on screen after screen after screen down the carriage I'm in. Keep watching when it restarts with the footage of Capital Day.

Or rather The Aftermath that triggered The Emergency we've had ever since.

Us bombing Them in payback. Them bombing Us with knobs on . . .

Capital Day – 12/4/12, like anyone needs reminding, turning buildings in all the major cities to craters.

Leaving injured people everywhere. Bloody. Dazed . . .

Or dead in one of the bodybags lined in front of M&S, Primark, Top Shop . . .

The screens on the train show CCTV of how everything happened city by city: London, Cardiff, Derry . . . And Guess What? When the film gets to the bit about Princes Street in Edinburgh on fire, our train *actually* pulls into *actual* Waverly Station and the screen I'm watching turns dark: shadowed out by the reflection of *real* Princes Street buildings.

Well, they're not proper buildings any more.

Ruins.

· Scott Monument with the top gone, like a big black wedding cake something's chomped a bite out of. And there's Jenners, the most famous store in the capital of Scotland, now a giant window frame with no glass and no sign.

Just the letters *'er'* hanging off the front of it to give you a clue what it's called.

You get shivers seeing something torn apart and burnt like that for real. Not just shrunk down to telly size. I can see all the way through Princes Street to the buildings behind on George Street.

'So civilised away from all the tourists on Princes Street,' Mum said *every* time we strolled along it. Well, *she'd* be strolling. *Isn't this lovely, Molly?* And I'll be like *Argggghhh! Speed up, Mum.* I mean, last time we came to Edinburgh we'd tickets for *Jacqueline*

Wilson at the Book Festival and Mum still wouldn't, couldn't, didn't hurry . . .

Sometimes Mum's *soooo* SLOW it drives me mad.

Take right now. *Finally*, we're chugging into the station, not quite stopped when we brake so suddenly I'm flung sideways. Donk! My head scuds the window-frame. An alarm drills through the train. It's loud enough to freeze my brain, but scary enough to make me want to sprint away from it.

Does it mean:

Bomb?

Gas?

Hijack?

Who cares?

Getting off's all that matters. Fast! Before every passenger surging from the carriages with their luggage squishes me and Mum and John into trainkill like poor Keith.

So I'm pressing the Doors Open button, ready to jump.

And what's Mum doing? Not what I scream at her: *'GET OUT!'*

She's tried to stand and gather herself together but ends up back on the floor doing spammy-mammy. John's trying to heave her upright but his backpack makes him top-heavy. When people start shoving against him he topples. Ends sprawled across Mum as the doors open – **BEEP BEEP BEEP BEEP** – and a flood of passengers trample them.

So here's me swept off the train. Hundreds of people shoving past because they think the train's going to *explode*.

Don't stand there. Run!

But I can't move, can I? I'm waiting for the two crouched shapes moving about in the gaps between boots and trousers and legs and shoes. I recognise John's arms, scrabbling to scavenge Mum's plastic bags. Some of them have already been kicked out on to the platform. One of them's fallen down between the train and the track. Think our sandwiches were in it, so there goes lunch for me and John.

At least the alarm stops ringing, though my ears make the announcement filling the station sound like it's being tannoyed through marshmallows:

ATTENTION. SCOTRAIL APOLOGISE FOR ACTIVATING THE EVACUATE SIGNAL ON THE GLASGOW TO EDINBURGH SHUTTLE. THIS WAS DUE TO A TECHNICAL ERROR . . .

'Oh, in the name of the wee man.'

Mum crawls off the train on her hands and knees. Dishevelled does not even half-describe the state of her.

'Sober up, missus,' some wiseguy from the train suggests as he sidesteps Mum and all her plastic bags.

'Oh, Molly. What am I like?' Mum asks, using my body to pull herself upright. When her face is level with mine she tries to kiss me, but I arch away.

'You're giving us a showing up,' I snap at her, stiffening my body. 'Why didn't you come off the train when I called you? I thought you were going to get crushed.' My voice cracks. 'You left me alone, Mum.' *And I was scared. And I don't want anything to happen to you. And I wish you were coming with me . . .*

My arms are still at my sides but when Mum folds hers round me, I just can't keep myself rigid any longer.

'I'd never leave you, Molly. We'll always have each other. In here. And here.' Softly, Mum punches her

33

heart. Then mine. Brings our heads together. 'Don't be scared, darlin',' she says like she can read my thoughts. And my anger melts and I sink against her.

6

Fuzzy-Felt Farm

Our Borders train is idling on a quiet platform. Ten minutes from now it leaves. Me and John leave.

Leave Mum.

Just as well Mum does her best to distract me by slipping into one of her annoying-even-though-she-means-well Mum routines.

'Toilet, Molly? Might not get chance again till Galashiels? You don't need to go? Sure? I'm going, anyway . . .'

When she comes back from the toilet she's wearing lipstick. She never wears make-up. This stuff's bright red.

And most of it's on your teeth, that snide voice inside my head nearly pipes up and I have to bite my tongue hard before I blurt it, because Mum's all bright bright smiles. Too bright.

'Hot dog, darlin'?' She offers me a steaming napkin. Another bright, bright smile. I shrug. 'No sandwiches?'

I'm remembering the tuna butties my Dad was making when I got up this morning. He kept glancing at me while he wrapped them.

'These should keep you and John going.'

Now, thanks to Mum's funny turn on the first train, my Dad's butties are squished under the Glasgow to Edinburgh shuttle. The thought of my Dad's wasted effort takes my own hunger and twists it. I even turn my nose up at the Curly Wurly Mum hands me just as I'm about to climb aboard the second train.

Don't exactly feel like eating. Or talking. Even to Mum. Even though the guard's signalling Mum off the platform and I don't know when I'll get to talk to her again. Instead I make myself stare at Mum's red lips because they're so unlike her. So not part of her. I watch them form words of goodbye to John.

'Look after, Molly. Do your best to keep in touch. We'll see you as soon as we can. Love you, son. Take care . . .'

Now the alien red lips are saying things to me but I

can't hear any of it. My head's pierced by a scream that could either be the guard's final whistle, or myself going 'Muuuum!!!!'

I don't hear normally again till the train's moving one way and Mum's face is blurring and shrinking away in the opposite direction. She's smiling. Bright. Bright. Eyes shiny. Waving me and John off with two hands now I'm holding all her plastic bags in mine. But Mum's lips are pale again, really pale. All that colour she added to cheer them up is thick and waxy on *my* cheek now. When I wipe it off with my hand it stains my fingers red.

'Oi, gonna stand there for the next two hours, Molly? Grab a seat and let's check what's in Mum's bags.'

John's beckoning me into an empty compartment where he's picked four seats with a table between them. A flask of tea rolls from the first of the plastic bags Mum handed me.

'Calm,' says John. Till he discovers we've no cups to drink from.

'What's Mum like, Molly?' he laughs and shakes his fist at the window.

'Have a black banana instead. *"Full of potassium. They're only a bit bashed,"'* John does Mum's voice.

'You're joking. They're mush. Shut up.'

The last thing I want to do right now is think of Mum, so even thought it's disgusting I make myself watch John attacking the bananas with the blades of a mini-fan Mum's randomly packed along with a battery-less radio and a handful of fridge magnets.

While John breaks the law by switching the batteries from our tox-tester into the radio, then fiddles for a decent reception, I search Mum's other bags. I wish I hadn't when I find the Thanks For Having Molly pressie Mum bought for me to give *Mrs Pearson, your temporary Mum*. That's what Mum chuckled two nights ago, sitting at our kitchen table, wrapping it up.

By the way, just in case you're one of these people always dying to know what's inside a parcel, calm down. Mum's wrapped three Yarrow's Shipyard tea-towels and a dire brooch made from a rabbit's paw set with a giant amethyst.

Kinda country and outdoorsy, Mum held the brooch against the slope of her chest before she wrapped it, angling it so it winked in the candlelight of the kitchen.

Sorta thing a farmer's wife might wear to a village Sale of Work. Think so, Molly? Mum asked me.

Sorta thing someone hands into a Sale of Work to ditch, my snide head-voice snorted so I shrugged. Imagined sending a vid-text of the brooch to Adele.

Er . . . Wood yr mum wr this???? !!!!
Mollyxx

Though what do I know about the sort of jewellery a farmer's wife wears?

Haven't given this Mrs Pearson a thought. Milk and electricity and telly and hot water. That's all she means to me. Only farmer's wives I've met live in Enid Blyton-world. Wear headscarves and aprons. Sell you eggs and ginger beer when you're on the run. They're stout and bustly. Jolly and stomp-abouty, like a country version of Mum, smelling of manure and apple pie instead of Oil of Olay. Mrs Pearson must be old too, I decide, drawing an empty circle on the train window. Adding apple cheeks. Button eyes. A frumpy headscarf. My Dad told us Mrs P could never have children.

That's what the doctors told Mum after John was born and before she started feeling she was going to have me when she was forty-five.

Bet Mrs Pearson's ancient too. Means her and Mum'll likely be pals if they ever meet up, I'm thinking as I huh enough air on the window to draw two bulky bodies side by side.

Then I rub one out.

Mrs P: what if she's strict? Makes me eat black pudding and liver? What if we don't get on? If she hates me? And I'm stuck with her, miles from home. With no phone connections to call Mum to come and get me . . .

I don't realise I've been biting my nails till John snatches my hand from my mouth and squeezes my fingers till I yelp.

'C'mere so I can keep an eye on you like Mum said.' John pulls me round the table to sit beside him. He crushes me against him with his big beefy drummer's arms.

'Everything's calm, Molly. You know Mum and Dad'd never send us anywhere crap,' John says, tucking my hair behind my ear and so he can hook one of his headphones on me.

Because John's trying to be decent and there's no way I'm going to cry in front of him, I force myself to quit imagining how ugly Mrs Pearson might be.

Instead I watch the landscape, building a virtual fuzzy-felt farm. I drop and drag anything I like the look of:

A smoking chimney.

A field of crows on corn.

A cottage wall crawling with roses.

Whorled haybales.

A lone horse grazing a paddock.

An emerald meadow flecked with sheep fluff.

A shamble of cows crossing a rutted lane . . .

SELECT.

Even though it's ages since I've used a computer, my mouse finger twitches when I see a collie sniffing a burn . . .

A strut of hens pecking a courtyard . . .

And you bet I click DELETE whenever my window fills with another lifeless windfarm. They're everywhere, and all the turbines have broken arms like the same vicious giant who scoffed the top off the Scott Monument in Edinburgh had the munchies here too. Some of the turbine arms are burned, left dangling on blackened cables, though mostly the arms have been ripped off then rammed into the earth, a reminder of why I'm on this train today:

The Emergency.

I shiver, sad for the crippled windfarms who used to wave while they made our telly and heat and light. In tribute, I stick a multicoloured musical turbine on my fuzzy-felt dream farm. It whirls along like a stripy seaside lollipop in time to the beat John's drumming to the tune we're sharing:

Here comes the sun . . .

Then suddenly John's voice cuts into my dwam. He's switching off the radio.

'This is it, Molly. All change . . .'

Will Nott and the Farmer's Wife

Wooo! Am *I* glad Mum's not here!

That's the first think I think when I clock the dog. See, Mum's completely terrified of dogs – right down to wee Jessie yappers. Mind you, even a major dog-lover like me would swither about asking *this* one to give Molly a kissy-wissy. Imagine a cross between Plug from the *Bash Street Kids* and the Hulk. Minus the looks. I'm not exaggerating when I tell you he – this dog's gotta be a he – is actually *drooling* while he strains to break the double-handed collar hold of a stocky man in a filthy orange boilersuit.

And he's growling. The dog, that is. Low, and not for show. Actually the man growls too.

43

'Shurrup, Snapper,' as he cuffs the dog and glares at me while I shoogle my wonkity cases down off the train. He keeps both hands on the dog's collar when he mooches towards me from the muddy pickup he's been slouched against. It's the only vehicle in sight.

Please don't let this be Farmer Pearson, I pray, exactly at the moment this man snarls, 'Fogarty!' and forces his way past me on to the train with Snapper. Either the dog or his master stink of booze.

'We're Fogarty,' I bleat.

'*Fogarty*,' the man growls louder, ignoring me. 'Labourer?' he shouts as John humpy-backed beneath his case and his backpack and his holdall, shuffles up the train.

'You're joking!' growly man complains to Snapper. He gobs at John's feet.

'Fogarty?'

John nods. 'Mr Pearson?'

'Will Nott. Move it,' Growly growls, cocking his head for John to follow.

'Will not move what?' John asks weakly, the sound of his voice making Snapper dive for his crotch.

'Hey, comedian here,' Growly snorts, kicking Snapper to heel. 'Step on it unless you want to walk ten miles. Both of you.' Growly jabs his finger at me then stomps towards the pickup.

'John, we can't . . . We're not . . . Mum wouldn't want . . .' I think I quaver but my words are sucked away in the slipstream of our train leaving the station. There's no going back.

'Room for one up front with me and Snapper,' Growly calls, revving his engine.

'Threat or invitation? I'll stick to the cheap seats.' John chucks our luggage into the back of the pickup. He helps me clamber over the tailgate before he joins me himself, muttering, 'Thanks a bundle for setting me up with a beam of sunshine, Dad.'

For the next twenty minutes the two of us hurtle on a journey that churns me sicker than anything me 'n' Adele've paid to ride in the Carnival. Even the two dead piglets jigging about the floor of the pickup look green.

I bury my face in my knees and pretend Mum's still hugging me like she did at the station when we said goodbye. Why did I ever let go of her? How can this be safer than staying in Glasgow, I ask myself as Growly suddenly veers off the road into a rutted field. He zig-zags every pothole so John topples on to me. Pinned between his rucksack and a rotting piglet I'm *desperately* trying not to pee myself as Growly accelerates towards a massive stone barn and . . .

'Gonk,' seethes John when Growly cuts the engine a hairsbreath from crashing. Wheelspins to a hand-brake stop.

'Will Nott, you're such an angel. Rushing my new girl over because you know how excited I am . . .'

OK. So I'm alive, and a lady's voice is breaking the silence in the back of the pickup. And I think she's talking about me. But in those moments after the pickup brakes, I can't move. I'm rigid, my fingers glued so hard to John's arm it'll take a crowbar to prise them free.

I can't see who's speaking. Just know it's not Growly, or Mr Will Nott as I'm realising he must be called. He's glaring into the back of his truck: beady black eyes, lips drawn back over yellow teeth. Snapper

46

beside him: beady black eyes, lips drawn back over yellow teeth . . . The dog's straining every sinew in his neck to reach John. And *Nott* in a smile.

'Snapper's not keen on you, son. Pity.' Mr Nott drops the tailgate. 'Better watch your fingers. And – oi – stay put, wide-o,' Mr Growly Nott growls, using his thick forearm to block John before he can jump from the pickup.

'You're mine, laughing boy. And we're not stopping. Work to do.'

'Not even time for a cup of tea, Mr Nott?'

There's the lady's voice again, though I smell Mrs Pearson before I see her. And in case you're wondering, she definitely doesn't smell of manure. Or wet dog. Or even apple pie.

I don't know what Mrs Pearson's perfume is, only that it's like a cloud of flowers. Light. Floaty. Sweet. Ooooh . . .

I can't help shutting my eyes when the smell wafts over me so I can drink it up my nose. When I open them again Mrs Pearson's at the foot of Nott's truck, smiling her head off.

And you know the first thing I think?

Not that she's beautiful. Which she soooo is.

Tall.

Slim.

Young, young, young compared to Mum.

Or that her frizzle's so *big* I wish I could vid-text Adele to show her right now:

Hey. 2 2 mega-peachy!!! Mollyxx

No, the first thing I think when I see Mrs Pearson is that – sorry, Mum – she'll *never* wear that dismal brooch I've to give her.

'Molly Fogarty! You've the happiest name!' Mrs Pearson leans her elbows on the pickup. She looks me up and down then claps her hands like I've just done something more wonderful than arrive.

'But you're pale,' she purses. 'Like you never see the sun, or eat fruit. Oh, time you started the Pernilla Programme. Fun, food, fresh air. And Pernilla's me by the way. Welcome to Paradise Farm, Molly.'

Pernilla: the name, one I've never, ever heard before, swirls in my head, mingling with the flower cloud smell of my new guardian.

Puh-nilla.

A greeny-blue name.

Tasting of peardrops dusted in icing sugar.

Puh . . .

A name that makes me think I'm stroking a pedigree cat.

A name that *must* have been invented specially for Mrs P: it suits her *soooo* perfectly.

'Pernilla.'

This makes me sound spammy but I say the name aloud. Wish I'd kept my trap shut. *Pernilla* turns Glasgow in my mouth.

'*"Purrrrnilllah"*,' John imitates my pronunciation, his mocking nudge sending me off the end of the pickup.

'Hi, Mrs Pearson, I'm John, Molly's brother,' he stretches out his arm from the truck, introducing himself in his most grown-up I'm-going-to-Yooni-to-do-Engineering voice.

But Pernilla doesn't seem to hear him.

'Molly, your accent. Love it! *Purrrrnilla*,' she copies me. Smiles. Then frowns. Wags her finger at me. 'But you mustn't be a *naughty* girl –'

'Too right, Molly. Remember what Mum said about manners,' John chips in. He's smiling at Pernilla, but she ignores him. She carries on talking to me.

'I just think calling me "Mrs Pearson" like your brother's done makes me sound *ancient*, Molly. I'm not, am I? So call me Nilly. It's younger. Friendlier.'

There's a snort from Snapper when Pernilla says *friendlier*. He lunges at John's arm before jumping back into the pickup, throwing Mr Nott a look that says: *Are we outa here?*

'Right, we'll be off, Mrs P. It's time city boy here got his hands dirty.' Growly slams shut the tailgate of the pickup on John and joins Snapper in the driver's seat.

'Thanks again, Mr Nott. Come with me now, Molly.' Pernilla's holding out her hand, walking away from Growly's van already. And without another glance at my brother I take it. Follow Pernilla inside.

I bet you're thinking: That's so mean of Molly. What a heartless cow, leaving John with that guy. And you've got a point. I let John drive away with a horrible man and his dog, and I don't say a proper goodbye and I don't know where he's going or when I'll next see him.

But, you have to see things from my point of view. First of all, I really, *really* need to pee. And secondly, because – phew – Growly Nott's not Mr Pearson, and Pernilla's *nothing* like the farmer's wife I imagined, I'm swamped with relief. So swamped that I can't worry that John's big cry of 'Everything's calm, Molly,' as Growly speeds him away sounds anything but.

Once I'm inside Paradise Farm for the first time I can't really think of anything but how uber-ultra-*peachy* everything is. I mean, I wash my hands in hot running water with liquid soap that smells like parma violets. My favourite smell. While I'm doing that I just catch a final glimpse of Growly's truck turning out the farm gate, but I'm more interested in the row of scented candles lined along Pernilla's window ledge to be honest. This is just Pernilla's *toilet* and it's amazing.

Why does Mum never buy anything that smells so good, I wonder. Mmmmm. The candles are spicy: pepper, ginger, lemon. They match the rug I'm standing on and the towels piled on a chair in size order. Why does *nothing* match at home in Glasgow? I could get used to this.

Hey Adele, R U jellus? Mollyxx

I imaginary vid-text, kneeling to scoop crimson petals from a huge bowl. I mean a bowl for nothing but petals! Back home, bowls in our cludgie catch drips from leaky pipes or steep wet laundry. Not here. I feel like I'm in a showhouse advert, deperate to see the rest of Paradise Farm now I'm not desperate to pee.

'Bet you can't *wait* to see your bedroom, Molly?' Pernilla says as soon as I open the toilet door.

She leads me down a long thick creamy carpet.

'Sitting room, study, bathroom. Explore yourself,' Pernilla says, moving fast, like she's as excited as I am.

'You're at the very end, Molly. Next to my room . . .'

Now, for one split second I almost ask Pernilla, *And where will John sleep tonight? Is Mr Nott's farm peachy as yours?* But then she reaches this door with **MOLLY'S ROOM** painted on it in gold lettering . . .

And quite frankly, I don't give two hoots about John's sleeping arrangements any more.

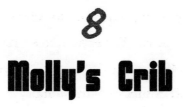

8

Molly's Crib

Because WOW! This peachy bedroom.

If I wasn't drivel at art I'd draw it. It's painted mermaid-scale shimmery like that nail varnish Adele's mum always wore on first dates till she met her Canada boyfriend and gave it to Adele: lilacypinkyplummy-purply.

'Iridescent paint. You like, Molly?' Pernilla asks when I touch a wall and don't speak.

'Hey,' Pernilla's concerned. 'We can change it. If it's too girly –'

Change it? Too girly?

Why redecorate perfect?

My curtains are layers of silk, star-sprinkled, same fabric as this canopy – yeah, *canopy* – draped over my bed. Is Pernilla psychic? How else could she know how much I *hatehatehate* sleeping in John's lumpy hand-me-down bunk with picked-off Narnia stickers on its headboard.

'You like, Molly?'

It's funny; Pernilla's holding a hand across her chest same as Mum does when she's spammy-mammy but unlike Mum, whose hips can't help bumping into things, Pernilla's swishing about, floaty like the curtains. She's switching on lamps, plumping cushions, explaining the all-in-one remote for my Very Own Telly and DVD like the one that my Very Own Mum refuses to let me have.

And my V.O. telly and DVD work! Everything works: the radiators are hot, my V.O. mini-fridge (three years on my Santa list, Mum!) is chill. Full of Cokes!!! Gold-dust is easier to find in Glasgow.

Even the computer boots up.

'Sorry. It's a dinosaur and there's no Internet, of course,' Pernilla apologises, 'but the desk's new. Phil built it. He can't *wait* to meet you –'

'Who's Phil? D'you mean Mr Pearson? Oh, wow this computer's got a camera! There's us.' I point at myself on the monitor and myself points back. Pernilla at my shoulder, her arm round me.

'Ooooh, where do I begin with Phil? Well, he's my other half. And guess what?'

Pernilla whispers behind her hand to my screen self. 'He's six years younger than me. I cradle-snatched him. Never had a girlfriend till we met because he works so hard on the farm. Day and night. We met on an Internet date – very naughty of me to be browsing,' she giggles, then adds more seriously, 'you should *never* do it yourself.' Pernilla leans even closer to the screen. 'Especially when you're about to marry someone else, like I was. But, I'm sorry. I'm totally impulsive and when I realised how much Phil was head over heels in love with me after one date . . . Though I shouldn't really be telling you any of this so soon. You'll think I'm a scarlet woman.' Pernilla smacks her hand. Then she leans her head against mine and sighs at the screen.

'Y'now. You'll love Phil, and he'll love you. He adores kids. He's just one of these guys who's born to be a dad and it's just so sad his Pernilla can't give him any babies when other people keep popping out children then don't look after them properly and . . .'

Well, there's plenty more on the subject of Phil and Pernilla and the babies she keeps trying for and some clock inside her ticking because she's thirty-eight now and all her little eggs are getting old. When Pernilla moves on to ugh stuff about fertility treatment, and sperm counts and the number of times she and Phil cuddle up in bed like lickle fluffy hamsters to make –

Believe me, I'm thinking *Too much information already*. Adele'd poke two fingers down her throat and gag if she heard half of the private stuff Pernilla spouts. And I know it's rude of me but I have to interrupt.

'You've years to have a baby. My Mum was forty-five when she had me so there's loads of time for you –'

'Ugh, I'm sorry but that's just –' Pernilla does a spammy-mammy hand-flap and looks as yucked-out as I'm feeling about what she's been telling me so far. I'm not meaning to dingy Pernilla or Phil, and it's sad that they can't have kids of their own, if that's what they want. But who wants to listen to baby-goo?

Change the subject, I'm willing Pernilla. *There's a bedroom from heaven to explore!* 'Anyway, I wanted everything perfect for you.' At last, Pernilla's talking my language again, showing off the walk-in wardrobe with its full-length mirror that Phil put up squint and Pernilla made him rehang. 'And if I'd known your size, I'd've bought clothes to welcome you.' Pernilla helps me shuck off my outside jacket, and my puffa and my school coat.

'We'll need to go shopping,' she trills (hey, suddenly I'm all ears again!), holding my jackets at arm's length the way you do when you're not sure what you're looking at but you're sure you don't like it. 'Coz there's so much fabby fashion for girls now I see how tiny you *really* are under all that gear . . .'

Pernilla breaks off to cover her mouth with her hands. 'Thought you might be one of those *big* girls, but you're not, thank goodness. I'd've had to disown you. Ooooh, I'm dreadful,' she giggle-whispers, opening a door next to the walk-in wardrobe. And I'm sorry if this makes you sick, but I've a second room the same size as my brand-new bedroom. Same iridescent

57

paint on the walls. Same silky curtains. No canopied bed though.

Just a bath. Oh yes! In the middle of the floor perched on lion's claws. There are two steps leading up to it. On one step are piled more towels than you'd find in our entire Fogarty family linen cupboard, and on the other sits soap, shampoo, body spray and . . . '*Bubble bath*,' I gasp when I see this giant Pernilla-coloured bottle. 'Can I use it? Is there enough . . . I mean, hot water?'

I'm unscrewing the bubble-bath lid. Sniffing – phwoah – a concentrated dose of flower-cloud smell. When I look up Pernilla's watching me, shaking her head like something's wrong.

So I think: *Oh well. I'm used to washing from a cold tap. At least my bedroom's peachy . . .*

Then Pernilla puts my hand over the hot tap and twists. Back home by this time in the afternoon there might be a rusty dribble if you're lucky, so the instant steam-facial I'm given is a shockarooney. But not as much the sight of Pernilla letting *gallons* of hot water disappear before she plugs the bath. Mum would need heart paddles if she saw the waste.

'Have as many baths as you like,' Pernilla waves her hand through the steam. 'Our reservoirs are full and we've had no power cuts so the Internet and phone lines being down are the only signs of The Emergency in Paradise. Enjoy yourself, Molly.'

'Thanks, everything's just so –' I start to splutter, but Pernilla puts her finger to my lips.

'Well, pay me back by letting me spoil you,' she smiles, cupping my cheeks with her hands. Then she adds something which, considering she's only met me an hour ago, is pretty extreme:

'Honestly, it's my dream come true to have a girl like you on Paradise Farm at last.'

9
Settling In

As soon as Pernilla leaves me I get steeping up to my neck in the first bath I've had since The Emergency made hot water rarer than emeralds in a lucky bag.

Don't ask me how long I wallow. All I know is John doesn't kick the door with a charming warning like: *You better let me in, Molly, I'm soiling my keks here!* and the only thing that forces itself into the room with me is the October sun. Lowered by the dusk it fills my private bathroom with goldy light. This catches the stars on my curtains, throwing their shadows on the walls where they glimmer till the sun dips behind the humps of faraway hills and the day dies.

I know this makes me sound like a tumshie but that moment when the daylight turns grey always makes me feel empty and strange. No matter where I am, no matter how much I'm enjoying myself, and even though I'm as good as thirteen, I need Mum near before I feel right inside.

All of a sudden I've homesickness surging up my throat like vomit. I'm out the bath, wriggling my jeans over wet legs. Hair dripping, I pad down Pernilla's thick carpet in bare feet.

'Hello?' I'm on the verge of tears, needing a cuddle I suppose. But when I find Pernilla in her kitchen, she lifts up my arm and twirls me round and round. Like I *look* as if I want to dance right now!

'*Here* she is,' Pernilla whoops as if there's a roomful of people here to greet me.

'Look at my new Molly. She's feeling wonderful and smelling *fantastic*, at last. Bet you're glad to get all your Glasgow germs washed off? You're brand new now.'

'I wonder how Mum's doing. I wish I could tell her I've arrived. Or speak to John. Maybe I could speak to John,' I say, my voice tiny. I suppose that explains why Pernilla doesn't seem to hear me. She's kind of hyper: excited, talking over me in a singy voice as she sits me down at her kitchen table. Stainless steel by the way, same as everything else in the room. Like the inside of a spaceship and totally not what you'd expect on a farm.

'Now. Dinner's on. Lasagne. You like? And fresh fruit salad. Late raspberries and strawberries. And homemade ice cream? Phil skims the milking –'

'My Mum would love all that but she can't eat cream. Give her skitters,' I say before I can stop myself.

'Sounds lovely, your Mum.' Pernilla pulls a face so full of distaste I find myself parroting exactly what Mum would say herself if she was here to explain away her dodgy stomach.

'It's not Mum's fault. It's her gall bladder. It's packed in now my Mum's fair and fat and over forty. "Actually well over forty" Mum always says.'

I shrug a smile at Pernilla but it's not returned. So I decide to tell her that joke Mum likes to tell against herself to show I'm not bothered about Mum being ancient.

'My Mum says everything goes to pot at her age: eyes, memory, waistline. So there's two things you never forget when you're over fifty. One,' I try to keep my face straight. In my head I hear Mum saying what I'm saying – only doing it better – wheezing so as not to chuckle before the punchline, 'You never pass a toilet. And two, you never trust a fart.'

Mum usually laughs till she cries when she tells this joke. Well, it *is* funny, *I* think so. But it must be a bit too clatty for Pernilla because she's not laughing. Fact, her mouth's turned down.

'Who told you that? That brother of yours?'

When I shrug my answer, 'Mum,' Pernilla tuts.

'Hmmm. Charming,' she sniffs. 'Let's dry your hair, Molly. It's dripping all over my floor.'

10
Nil and Phil

'You know, I think we look quite alike, Molly.'

'Everyone says I'm the double of my Mum. Even though she says she's double my size.'

'Oh, poor thing. That must be embarrassing. For you, I mean. I'd *hate* that.'

Pernilla's behind me. We're both facing my full-length mirror. 'Well, I think you look like me. Apart from this *mop*, Molly! When in goodness was the last time your Mum took you for a trim?'

Ouch!

Pernilla's brushing down my hair from my parting instead of working up from the ends. I want to show her Mum's pain-free technique, but Pernilla looks so pleased and dreamy-faced doing what she's doing: brush, brush, brushing like I'm her favourite doll getting a new do, I let her get on with it. Try not to squeak.

'This isn't hurting, Molly?' asks Pernilla, digging the brush into my scalp. 'You know, your hair's nearly the same colour as mine.'

I'm in agony here, eyes brimming, but I nod, 'Mmmm.'

'Oh you think so, too?' Pernilla quits brushing.

Halleluia!

She presses her head against my ear.

'Think, if you'd a frizzle, we could be twins?'

'Not allowed a frizzle,' I shrug.

Pernilla sighs and shakes her own curls like I've just told her someone *died*. Before I know what I'm saying, I'm wearing a petted lip and telling Pernilla, 'Or pierced ears. Or a puppy.'

Pernilla cups my chin in her hands. 'Sweetheart, *everyone's* frizzled in the whole world. And what's wrong with two tiny holes in your ears? Sounds like that old Mum of yours should drag herself out the Noughties.' Pernilla's eyes are smirky, like Adele's when she wants me to laugh while Miss Squishbutt's giving me yet another bollocking for carry-on.

Pernilla's about to say more when there's a knock at my door. 'Everybody decent?'

Now, OK, I know you'll be thinking: imagine Molly being surprised that *Farmer* Pearson looks like a *farmer*. Adele would be rolling her eyes. '*Hu-llo*'. But the point is, does Pernilla seem one bit farmer's-wifey? Uh-uh. She's totally *urban* and pulse. So seeing Mr Pearson's big farmery face burst through the magazine perfectness of Paradise Farm's like finding a pin-up of a tractor in *Closer*. Without being rude about him – because he's not ugly and his smile is *massive* – he looks like he could do with a dod of Mum's Oil of Olay even if he's no way old enough to have ultra-mature skin. But it's raw and red and rough like Pernilla puts him outside all day no matter the weather. His hair's red and rough too, poking out a beanie and so shaggy I can't tell what's straw and what's not. He smells funny too: of cold air (sweet) and animals (OK) and dung (so-so) and sweat (hmmmm). The combination's not *nasty*, but it's sharp, clashing with the floweriness of Pernilla. And when Mr Pearson steps into my room with one muddy boot – *whooofff* – believe me: he overpowers Pernilla's perfume *completely*.

'Hi.' Mr P's offering me the biggest hand I've ever seen, streaked with the kinda brown muck I don't want to analyse. I like him immediately because when he smiles his eyes crinkle up and remind me of John.

'Don't panic, Nil. Know I haven't washed. Just wanted to meet Molly. Phil,' Mr Pearson keeps his hand outstretched. I reach to shake but Pernilla shoos him away.

'You know the drill, Phil. Scrub-a-dub,' Pernilla singsongs, closing the door in Phil's face. She picks up a hairdryer. Turns it on me full blast. Hot.

Boss of her man, that one, Mum would be commenting out the side of her mouth to me if she was a witness to this little scene.

Oooh, get her! John might camp it up if he was here.

But he's not. They're not. Or my Dad, I think, forcing myself to enjoy the attention Mum would never pay to fluffing my hair crazy like Pernilla does to make it look more like hers.

'I'm sorry. You just *have* to get a frizzle, Molly.'

Before dinner she rakes through my clothes.

'Oh. My. God, Molly Fogarty. It's not your fault, but

this is all tragic! I know there's a war on in Glasgow, but surely Top Shop's still open? Honestly, someone needs to give your Mum a bit of a lesson in what girls your age should be wearing!'

'But I've plenty pulser outfits,' I interrupt. 'There wasn't room in my cases –' I defend my wardrobe and Mum, when Pernilla silences me.

'Girl, you need a total fashion makeover. And you're going to get it.'

What can I say to that? Not a lot, since Pernilla's brushing my lips with gloss that tastes of cherries.

'Keep it, Molly,'

She mascaras my eyes silver.

'You're never too young for bling.'

And paints my nails green. Same as hers.

'Look at *you*!' Pernilla giggles, twirling me all the way up her hall.

'Look at *you*!' I can imagine Mum saying if she saw me now, tarted up like this. She wouldn't be giggling.

11

Dinner is Served

Just before dinner I present Pernilla with Mum's Thanks For Having Molly Gift. For a joke I carry it into the kitchen balanced on top of a mountain of squashed bog roll like it's a jewel on a cushion of silk.

Pernilla examines the brooch without taking it out of its box.

'Mum says it's just a token, and if you don't like it, I'll change it when I go back to visit –'

'You can never have enough teatowels, can you, Molly?' Pernilla smiles, shutting her gifts in a drawer. Which I think's a bit rude, actually. Maybe she's one of these people who don't like getting presents. Adele's a bit like that. Fussy. Anyway, I'm glad Mum's not here to see what Pernilla's done. Because she'd be hurt, I think to myself when I'm shooed from the kitchen.

'Off you pop to the dining room. Wash your hands on the way.'

'Bit perjink' Mum would call this set up. Me, sitting at one end of a glass table all busy with fancy crystal and too much cutlery. The dining room's dim and low ceilinged. Maybe all dining rooms are like this. I wouldn't know. Back home our dining room's the kitchen recess and the only other dining room I've ever eaten in was in school. It honked of cabbage and boiled custard and was full of boys and girls and noise . . . Used to anyway, I think, shivering as I recall how the diners kept dwindling over the last few months. What happened to some of them?

Or maybe I'm just shivering because Pernilla's dining room feels chilly, like it's not used much. Plus I'm starving.

'Could eat a scabby tabby,' I hear Mum's voice chuckling in my head. If she was beside me, she'd be nudging me. *But you're not.* I have to chew my lip so as not to cry when Pernilla and a scrubbed-up Phil carry in bowls of soup.

'Homemade. Spinach and courgette. Eat up,' Pernilla tells me pointing at my bowl of swirly green liquid. But I can't. There are four spoons at my place. All different shapes and sizes. I don't know which one to lift without looking like a spud.

'Nilly's been polishing the family silver in your honour. Don't ask me what's wrong with the stuff we usually use,' Phil interrupts my misery. He's holding a fat, round spoon up to my face to show me my reflection. When he dips it in his soup I pick up the same spoon and copy him and keep dipping, till my bowl's empty.

'Looks like snot, but tastes great, eh Molly?' Phil winks as he leans back in his chair, smacking his belly.

You're dead like John, I'm about to tell him when Pernilla tuts, 'Phil, really. Why are men so vulgar?'

'What, Nilly?' Phil belches. He grins at me and the green streaks of spinach and courgette soup at the sides of his mouth smile too.

'I've never tasted anything like that before –' I look round the table, feeling much better now.

'Oh, doesn't your Mum cook? That'll be why you're

71

so pale –' Pernilla sighs before I'm finished what I was saying.

'My Mum makes brilliant soup, but never creamy because if she eats rich food she gets the trots and –'

'Let's just change the subject, can we? I think I've heard enough about your Mum's intestines for one day.'

Pernilla's on her feet. She claps her hands then whisks the soup bowls away.

'Open the champagne now and fill, Phil,' says Pernilla, serving me lasagne before anyone else.

'Mum says I'm not allowed wine.' I put my hand to the top of my wine glass.

'Oh for goodness' sake. What your Mum doesn't know won't hurt her. I won't tell if you won't.' Pernilla pulls my hand from the glass with her long, cool fingers, 'And anyway, this is a special occasion,' she beams into my face like I'm the Best Thing since the Solar Ipod Earphone-Shuffle. Which I'm not. I'm just Molly. Taking in Pernilla's promises. They're making my head spin before I've even *sipped* my champagne.

'Tomorrow I want to shop you till you drop. Spoil you rotten and –'

'Ahem,' Phil interrupts. He's holding out the flat of his hand to Pernilla, same as random-search officers do when they want to check your bags in town.

'Calm down, Nilly. You're getting carried away,' Phil says gently, shaking his head at Pernilla and raising his glass to me. 'Welcome,' he toasts me, 'though I hope you're back home with your Mum and Dad by Christmas –'

'That's nice, Phil,' Pernilla's beaming, but not in a pleased way. Squishbutt's the only other person I've ever seen who can pull off that face trick. 'Molly's only just *here* and you're wishing her away. *I'll* make a toast.'

Pernilla's on her feet, holding her champagne to my mouth so I have to glug.

'Molly, I hope you're soooo happy here, you *never* want to leave.'

'Don't worry, I won't if you serve up meals like this every day!' I gasp when Pernilla plonks this massive bowl of *fresh* fruit in front of me and takes away my empty lasagne plate.

'Help yourself, Molly,' she invites. Like I'm not already digging ice cream through a mountain of not-tinned raspberries and strawberries. First I've seen for *months*.

'Slovely,' I splutter, scoffing all my raspberries before I lift my head. Taking seconds. Habit, not just greed makes me do this. I've always gobbled raspberries *instantly* if John was around, else he'd snaffle my portion. I can't help myself giggling at the thought of John's face seeing me guzzle like this. He'd be *green* as Pernilla's snot soup with jealousy.

'What's so funny, Molly?' asks Pernilla.

'See John. He'd be drooling if he was here,' I tell her.

'Really,' Pernilla sniffs. 'That's boys for you.' She chases a raspberry round her plate, not looking at me. 'Bet you're glad he's out your hair for a while. He'll need to mind his manners with Mr Nott.'

'You can say that again. I hope the lad's all –' Phil's frowning at Pernilla.

All what? I'm thinking.

'Oh, he looked like he could handle himself, Phil.

Maybe you could clear up now, darling?' Pernilla taps my hand like she wants to change the subject. Though I'm not quite ready.

'But *when*'ll I see John again?'

'Oh. Farmer Nott'll be keeping him too busy for socialising. And we're going to be even busier. It's a good few miles to his place, you know. We can't use up petrol unless we have to. But soon. You'll see John soon.'

'Good stuff.' Phil's heading for the door, his arms piled with plates when he catches me yawning.

'Maybe you fancy an early night, Molly. Long day,' he smiles. I stand up. Nod.

'I'll give you a hand with the dishes, then go to bed,' I tell him but Pernilla tugs me back down into my seat.

'Behave yourself,' she shoos Phil away. 'Clearing up's Phil's job and *we're* just getting to know each other. I won't keep you long,' Pernilla promises. Then she giggles.

'Guess what? I'm going to be your new teacher on Monday. You'll have to call me Mrs Pearson. I'll feel as old as your – What's your Mum called, again?'

'Kitty,' I tell Pernilla.

'Yes, I'll feel as old as your Mum. Kitty. That's quite an old-fashioned name these days, isn't it? Think I'll just call her *Mrs F* . . . if I ever have to meet her.'

Pernilla leans close to me and whispers even though it's just us in the room.

'It wouldn't feel right for me to call your Mum *Kitty* since she's . . . well . . . quite a bit older than . . . And to have a girl your age. Must be weird sometimes. With your friends . . .'

Pernilla's eyes are all over my face. Shining. Darting. Probing. And I know. I just know. She's wanting me to tell her things.

About Mum.

And I *could* tell her about the time me 'n' Mum 'n' Adele were standing on a bus into Glasgow on a Saturday. Jam-packed it was. A bloke made a boy shift off the seat for the Elderly and Infirm. Give it to Mum.

Adele was raging. Pretended she wasn't with me the rest of the journey.

And the other time I was trying clothes in Top Shop

and I heard the shop-assistant asking Mum: *Does your granddaughter needed another size*? Never told Adele.

Sometimes it's embarrassing, my mouth's tempted to blurt at Pernilla. But so what? I love Mum all the same. Whatever. And tonight I'm not going to be able to tell her that to her face. Hear her whisper back as she kisses me.

You too, darlin'. Always.

'Mum's the best.' I frown like I don't understand what Pernilla's getting at, because inside my chest I feel this sudden tug of pain. Feels like there's an invisible rope attached to me and Mum. And it's just been yanked.

'Course she is. Naughty Nilly!' Pernilla smacks her hand.

12

Rose-tinted Morning

D'you ever wake up and you don't have a clue where you are or how you got there? Well that's how my first morning on Paradise Farm began. One minute I'm dreaming I'm cooried up warm next to Mum in her bed and she's snoring gently in my ear. The next someone who's not Mum is trilling, 'Wakey-wakey, Princess Molly,' and instead of de-velcroing the blackout from my window two floors up, is swooshing my curtains apart to dazzle me with rose-tinted daylight and a view of sheep-specked hills.

I can only hope it was Pernilla and not Phil who sleepwalked me from the dining room to my new bedroom last night, since whoever put me to bed also went to the bother of folding my clothes neatly at the foot of the bed and then – *yikes* – undressing me. I check to see it's still the same me in my underwear because the space above my head is sprinkled with silver stars and my hands are tangled in silky fabric that shivers me when it rubs together.

Everything's so different from home, I'm thinking, as Pernilla swishes through my room in a purple dressing gown. She's opening my drawers, my wardrobe, matching up clothes.

'Up, up, up, Molly,' she sings, the complete opposite of Mum first thing in the morning. She can't open her eyes till she's had a cuppa, let alone swish. And as for the dressing gown *she* slumps around in back home: if I tell you it ties with pulley rope you'll get the gist.

But you won't even be up and about yet, Mum. It's Sunday. You'll be having a lie-in before church. My Dad doing a fry-up if we've anything to fry-up, while I sneak in beside you and we listen to your golden oldie Jonathan Ross show on the radio . . .

Funny. Everything's bright as new paint and shimmery fresh here at Paradise Farm, but it fades to blankness when my mind takes me home. I'm miles and miles away till Pernilla shakes me back into my new routine.

'No more dozing. We'll grab breakfast on the way, coz we need to hit all those shops in Carlisle running.'

Pernilla's not joking.

'We've been away all day. My Mum gets wiped out after a couple of hours in town,' I gasp as Pernilla's Mini swings into the courtyard of Paradise Farm.

'Well you've traded her in for a younger model now. And hey, doesn't time just race when you're having fun, Molly? *Buy this. Buy that.'*

Pernilla reaches to squeeze my hand.

'But you've bought me so much.'

Too much, I hear Mum's voice in my head. Picture her taking in all the jackets, trousers, belts, bags, boots, tops, bras and *new* knickers (thank phew!). I've never been so spoiled in my life! Something from *every* shop we went into. Pernilla insisted. *Way too much*, I hear Mum's voice again. This time it makes my stomach tumble its wilkies. Because this is the first time I've given Mum much thought since this morning.

'Soon as I get in I'm going to write to Mum. Tell her I'm OK. It's so weird not just being able to talk to her,' I tell Pernilla.

'But you can talk to me instead. I wouldn't rely on snail-mail these days, anyway. Telegrams are the only reliable way to send messages in a hurry. Or an emergency. Wanting a chat with your Mum's hardly that when I'm here.' Pernilla squeezes my hand again. This time I draw mine away.

'I'm still writing.'

'Well, come say hi to Phil first. He'll think we're lost.'

Instead of stopping at the farmhouse Pernilla drives past. She heads for the fluorescent brightness of the milking parlour.

'This way,' Pernilla beckons me from the car. And even though I'm thinking too much of Mum and my Dad and what they're doing right now to chat to Phil, I follow Pernilla. I've a kind of feeling she'd be miffed if I don't.

So I watch her kiss Phil and sigh, 'Oh, honey. I've had the best day ever with my girl. Don't I look as if I've had the best day?'

Then I let Pernilla introduce me to Phil's 'other women': all fifty of the brown-eyed, long-lashed cows being electronically milked by two men in overalls. I'd say both of them look older than my Dad but Pernilla calls them 'The dairy boys: Tom and Jack –'

'Not to confused with the *other* dairy boys who should be mucking in here too. I'm Tom,' nods the dairy boy nearest to me.

'Aye. You won't meet the *real* boys. One's my grandson, Jack, same as myself. Soldier now, isn't he, Beauty? Him and his pal.' Jack is staring hard at the nearest cow. He's breathing heavily, his mouth open and turned down. For a moment time seems to stop in the dairy. Then Phil shakes Jack's sleeve. He mutters something to him but I don't catch it because Pernilla suddenly grabs my hand.

'Hey lookie, boys,' She twirls me up and down an aisle of blinking, stinking cows.

'Now *I've* a beautiful girl of my own to spoil like you spoil your girls in here. Isn't she the *best*?'

When none of the dairy boys – Phil included – abandons the cows they're tending to admire my new fashion flack jacket and ForcesUKstyle combats, Pernilla tries the ladies.

'Honestly Gertie, if you'd *seen* the outfit Molly arrived in yesterday you wouldn't believe this is the same girl,' she whispers in the twitching ear of one. To another, who, by the way, is right in the middle of plopping out a steaming cowpat, she giggles behind her hand, 'Between you and me *that* says it all about Molly's Mum's fashion sense.'

I can't help myself giggling along with Pernilla, but nor can I help myself blurting, 'Nilly, please can I go and write to Mum now.'

I start my letter as soon as I'm back in the farmhouse. Even before I try on my new clothes.

Dear Mum and Dad – *hey! Look. I'm typing on a P.C. Remember them?*

Spellchecked and everything!!! I'M TRYING MAD FONTS FOR A LAUGH.

Hope you can read them.

Sorry if you don't get this. The post's

rubbish. Mrs Pearson thinks I shouldn't even bother writing. SAYS she'll telegram in an emergency. Mum, HONEST, she's so peachy because she took me shopping for new clothes all day but she makes me call her Nilly!!! That feels funny but she'll be back to Mrs Pearson again when she's my teacher. Oh dear, that's soon.

We get Corrie on telly here. Mum, d'you want me to watch so I can tell you what's happening even though the telly's in my room and you don't approve??? Guess what? I've a fridge in my room, too. SO NOW I FORGIVE YOU FOR FORGETTING TO TELL SANTA I WANTED ONE. Ha ha.

Guess what more? LAST NIGHT I ATE GREEN SOUP WITH CREAM. NO, I WASN'T SICK BUT I TOLD NILLY ABOUT YOUR GALL BLADDER. THINK THAT WAS <u>WAAAAY</u> 2 MUCH INFORMATION. SHE'S A BIT POSH ABOUT FARTS AND STUFF. BUT HER HUSBAND'S NOT. HE'S SCOTTISH AND HE'S COW-MAD – KISSES THEM AND

EVERYTHING!!! BUT HE'S PEACHY. FARMER PHIL, THAT'S HIM. HE'S NOT THE FARMER JOHN WENT TO. He's Nott – he was totally evil!!! and he picked us up from the station with a dog you'd have died off if you'd seen, Mum.

But Phil's decent. His proper dairyboys joined ForcesUK AND HE'S LEFT WITH TWO ANCIENT MEN LIKE NEARLY DAD'S AGE TO HELP HIM. (KIDDING about ancient ha ha) Dad, why couldn't you have sorted John work with Phil instead of Farmer Nott? He'd have learned to snog a cow – good practice for the ugs he dates! I might ask Phil to give John a job but I don't think Nilly would like it. Doesn't seem to like boys – don't blame her, Ha Ha – and she'd have to buy John what she bought me and that would rook her. There's an an extra bedroom here. Maybe you both can visit . . . Pleeeze!!! Gotta go now. School tomorrow – oh no!!!!

Anyway, hope you get this letter. Pernilla

says she'll post it for me.
WRITE, WRITE, WRITE AND SAY WHEN I
CAN C U . . .
MISSING YOU ALREADY
MOLLY XXXXXXXXXXXXXXXXXXXXXXXXX
XXXXXXXXXXXXXXXXXXXXXXXXXXXXXX
XXXXXXXX

13

Teacher's Pet

At six-thirty next morning I'm wishing I'd slipped myself into that envelope Pernilla said she posted off to Mum and my Dad. Means I could have zedded all the way to Glasgow. Instead I'm woken when Pernilla bursts into my bedroom trilling, 'Good morning, my new pupil!' till I slur 'Gmuh' back.

Then I'm presented with a *huge* glassful of dairy-fresh calcium (tepid milk straight from Gertie-moo's nether regions!). Told, 'Drink up, snoozy Suzy!' and advised my bath and breakfast are waiting.

Forget washing. I can hardly open my eyes. And as for eating the 'healthy Scottish breakfast' Pernilla wants me to down on top of unpasteurised milk! Forget that too!

'Do I have to go to school today?' I bleat in the *Ifeelsick* voice that usually tricks Mum. Unfortunately

Pernilla's too busy being a morning person to notice how allergic to Mondays I am.

'So,' she quizzes me while I play with my porridge. 'I know your Mum isn't a teacher like me but I suppose she tried to keep up with work you missed. Y' know? When your school closed?'

'She tried,' I shrug, 'but we always got fed up. She hates maths and she's even worse at sums than –'

'Oh. So Mum hasn't been helping you. That's *awful*.'

It's not that awful! Suits me, I'm thinking as Pernilla rests her hands on mine and squeezes and sighs and tuts like she feels really sorry for me, or something.

'So what d'you need to catch up with most? English? Maths? Both?'

I'm not joking, before we even reach Valley Juniors I feel as if I've sat a day of orals no one told me to study for.

Much worse – and Adele would totally disown me for life if she saw *this* – is me walking hand in hand into class with a *teacher* – even if Pernilla is pulse and peachy. My face is blazing like I'm allergic to classrooms when Pernilla raises my arm and waves it about like a flag of surrender to catch the attention of a roomful of strangers. 'Upper Juniors.' she announces, 'Say hello to Molly Fogarty all the way from Glasgow –'

'Hello Molly *Fo*-garty,' chime five girls with instant obedience. Their row of desks is practically touching Pernilla's and, without seeming to blink, they beam into her face like they want to *eat* her. All of them have mega, Pernilla-copy frizzles so bulbous they mesh like stripes in a multicoloured itchy-wool scarf: blonde, ginger, black, mousy, chestnut. None of them budge their eyes from Pernilla to even glance at me. Who cares, they look like gonks, well younger than I am, I decide, checking out the row behind. It's worse. Four boys. Small and wriggly. Noses running. All ignoring me too. I can understand why. The smallest boy's spinning two upside-down dead mice on his desk. At least I think they're dead . . .

'Did you say *Dolly* Foghorn, Missus Pear-*son*?' chimes another boy who looks *far* too old to be a pupil at Valley Juniors.

Suddenly I'm wishing I'd checked a mirror for sleep crumbs in my peepers before I left the farm.

Cyoot, Adele? u think? Mollyxx

His voice sounds Irish. *Is he another evacuee like me*? I wonder, trying to scope this guy without looking, if you catch my drift. His hair's jet black, long and tumbly and his smile's wicked. Dimply like John's and . . .

'*Molly*, Fergal Lyons,' snips Pernilla. 'While I hear the other boys reading – yes *reading*, so put your mice away, Mark Jones – you can show Molly your jotters.'

'Snotters, my pleasure?' Fergal Lyons leers at Pernilla. He's twisting both index fingers at the entrance to his nostrils. I want to laugh but Pernilla flinches then shudders, '*Jotters*. Now,' and glides towards the girls in the front row, her voice softening like butter in a microwave, 'Poor Molly's been through some *very* hard times because of The Emergency. She's not led as fortunate a life as some of us recently and her mother's sent her to live with me to have a better –' Pernilla burbles so gravely about hardships I know nothing about that the Frizzle girls tilt their heads and prop each others' hairdos up in sympathy.

What's she on about? I've a brilliant life in Glasgow apart from The Emergency, I'm about to guff, but before

I can speak Pernilla proclaims, 'But best of all Molly can have uninterrupted schooling now. Won't she, girls?'

'Yes, Miss-us Pear-son,' the Frizzle girls chirrup while Pernilla steers me through the classroom to a desk beside Fergal.

'So you want me to take care of the poor soul, Miss?' Fergal asks Pernilla, shaking his curls sadly. 'Come and sit here, Dolly Foghorn.' He pats the empty chair beside him, his eyes blinking kindly at me while his mouth struggles not to smirk.

'*I'll* be taking care of Molly, thank you. You just show her where you are in maths,' Pernilla snaps at Fergal. Then she shoogles my shoulders like she's limbering me up for a workout.

'Molly's desperate for brainwork, so none of your time-wasting.' Her eyes narrow on Fergal.

Oops. Is Pernilla in for a dissy! Deciding I'm one of those insane cabbages who LIKE learning. Wait till she sees how I tackle sums and spelling.

Soon as I sit down Fergal nudges me in the ribs. Opening the back cover of his maths jotter, he sighs,

91

'Wish I was teacher's pet like you, Foghorn. I work *so* hard for her. 'Specially at art. See –'

Well, I assume it's Pernilla he's drawn. Matchstick body, balloon boobs (that's just *totally* boys) and a humungous frizzle. There are birds nesting in it.

It's so outrageous I clamp my hand over my mouth before I gut myself laughing, *This is more like it*, I'm thinking. Back to Ye Goode Olde Days. Me 'n' Adele. Back row of the class. Chance for a decent carry on so I don't die of arithmetic . . .

'Hey. Lend us a red pencil for your face, I'll do you too, Foghorn,' Fergal whispers. He's already writing *Teacher's Pet* at the top of a blank page.

So I shrug, 'OK.' Smile into his eyes. Green like my favourite colour they are. Twinkly. Sweet for a gonk-boy . . .

Behave yourself, Molly, I'm thinking.

'But I'll draw you first,' I simper. Then I wrestle Fergal's pencil from his fist and his jotter from his desk. Draw a matchstick body with a bum for a face. A spotty hairy one, complete with fart clouds wafting off it.

'Everything all right, Molly?' Pernilla glowers at

Fergal, her Mrs Pearson radar catching the scuffle of paper.

'Perfect, Miss,' I twinkle, kicking hard at Fergal's ankle.

'We're working away. Dolly's catching on grand,' grins Fergal. 'By the way,' he whispers to me, 'd'you've a brother with dyed hair and a big long coat?'

Taken aback, I nod. 'John.' I'm grinning at Fergal but he shakes his head, his face grim.

'Thought you look related. I stay over in the next field. We talk. He's not getting on too well with –'

'Not getting on too well with *what* exactly, Mister Lyons?' Pernilla interrupts. She plants herself in front of Fergal with her arms folded till we both put our heads down and start writing.

14
First-class Secret

'Can you believe it's only been three weeks? Feels like we've lived together forever. You think, Molly?'

'Mmmm,' I nod and grin though mainly I'm grinning because I can't get over sitting in First Class on a Carlisle to Glasgow train with Pernilla. We're being served free drinks and shortbread.

'These seats are *massive* and they recline and vibrate. Wait till I tell Mum. Hope she's at the station. Can't wait to see her –'

Pernilla interrupts with a yawn.

'Well, *I* just hope we get back to Phil in one piece,' she says, pursing her mouth at the view from the window where the fields and hills of the Scottish Borders have given way to the industrial estates and high-rises and gap sites and factories on the outskirts of Glasgow.

We'renearlyhome. We'renearlyhome. We'renearlyhome, clacks the train.

'Dismal,' Pernilla sighs. 'I hope my telegram arrived and your mother knows we're coming. I don't fancy rambling the murder capital of Scotland on a Friday night with a child –'

Pernilla's turned so glum, I do my best to reassure her: 'I'm not a child and I know how to get home if Mum's not waiting but she will be. Anyway, Glasgow's no more scary than any other big city,' I promise, adding, 'That's what Mum says.'

'Ooooh, feel *much* better now,' Pernilla mutters to the window so I'm not quite sure if she's being sarky or not. 'When I offered you a weekend treat, Molly,' she goes on without looking at me, 'I was thinking we'd have a day in a spa or invite all the girls in class for a sleepover. Imagine you choosing an endurance trip to the battlefields of Scotland!'

'But I haven't seen Mum and my Dad for ages. And it won't be that bad. We get water from the street and use candles and light the camping stove . . .'

I can hear my voice turning small as I wonder if

asking Pernilla to bring me home was a bad idea. The problem is, when she promised 'Choose *anything* you want to do this weekend, Molly. Your wish is my command,' it was the only thing I thought of. And I'm almost insulted she could imagine I'd pick a night with the Frizzle girls and their pony chat over a visit to Mum and my Dad. That would be torment, not treat. I'd rather be blown by shrapnel to Uranus!

'Molly, lighten up. I'm teasing you. I'll survive two nights. Used to be a Girl Guide. I can slum it,' Pernilla's giggly again. Thank goodness.

'Anyway, I'm curious. It's time I met your Mum. I want to know why you're so behind in schoolwork. Find out what you've been taught up in Glasgow. When it comes to spelling you and that Fergal Lyons are clueless.'

Fergal. At the mention of his name I feel my cheeks heating up.

'But Fergal's decent.' *The only decent thing about Valley Juniors*. I smile, more to myself than to Pernilla, because I can picture Fergal smiling back at me – dimples, freckles, cheek – till Pernilla's finger waggles the image away.

'That boy's an utter pest who wouldn't even *be* in my class if he hadn't fallen back too far for secondary school –'

Fallen back. Thicko! I'm mentally rehearsing how I can slag Fergal when I next see him till Pernilla adds, 'He didn't cope well after his mother was killed –'

Killed? 'I didn't know.' I gasp.

'Mmmm. Caught in a nail bomb out shopping in Derry on Capital Day. Fergal and his dad – he's some kind of hippy who builds chess sets or something useless – they left Ireland after that. New start. Rented a cottage and workshop near Mr Nott's place. Back of beyond.'

'That's really sad,' I gulp, asking myself if knowing Fergal's mum's dead changes how I feel about him. Do I like him more? Or less? Do I feel sorry for him? Would I still have scratched

Shrek + Miss Piggy = F.L.

down the front of his spelling jotter?

Probably.

After all, he did ask me last week if my blackheads made good pets. What I fed them.

97

And worse than that, only this morning in class he'd the cheek to offer me updates on John and pass messages between us . . .

In exchange for kisses!!

'Get real, green eyes!' I snarled when he puckered his lips out and jigged about in front of me waving a letter.

'Oh no! Your fly is down, sadcase,' I lied loudly enough to make the Frizzle girls gawp at him. While he was busy blushing like a giant red Smartie I snatched the letter and strutted into the girls' toilets. Ha Ha.

Mind you, minutes later I wasn't laughing. When I read John's letter I felt sick to the pit of my belly. It went:

Guess Who?

Howz it going? Betyer missing me nearly as much as I'm missing my drumkit.

First things first. If you're reading this letter
you have to kiss Ferg. Promised him you would. Go on. A biiiig wet slobber for me! Ferg says

you know you wanna . . . Have you? Awww, poor Ferg's turned into frog now. Ha Ha.

Anyway, I'm writing this letter so you can tell Ferg and he can tell me how Mum and Dad're doing coz I hear you're going home this weekend, you jammy sponge-cake. Will you do that, Mols? Check the folks're Calm and tell Ferg coz it's cracking me up not seeing them and I know Mum'll be stressing herself thin about me too.

By the way, I spotted you out shopping with your Ice-Queen in Galashiels last week both togged-up like kid-on soldiers in the same pulse gear: the creepy twins!!!! You didn't see me??? Ya sure??? I was loading Nott's pickup with beer (not for yours truly, alas) and I saw you and I was waving like crazy and calling your name. Your Mrs P looked over – and I SWEAR she clocked me, but she whisked you up a side street and I couldn't get away from Nott to follow.

Anyway, since you're into dressing up like

a soldier of fashion, I've an undercover mission for you: please find out when we're going home. I mean, we're here three weeks now and honest, Mols, I'm finding it tough, BUT DON'T TELL MUM THAT, OK??? I promised her I'd stick this job to dodge ForcesUK so don't show her this letter. Just find out when I can SPLIT!!! See, I can't get a day off, and I'm even starting to miss you, smelly.

I know Dad'll argue farm work beats catching a bullet in some foreign country but I bet I'd be treated better under some sadist-sergeant in the bloody desert. See, this joker Nott is Nott A Nice Man. Seriously, I'm *99%* tempted to take the king's shilling . . .

Nott has me mucking out his pigs and they're sick, crapping rings round themselves. Nott does Nott himself. Just shouts a lot. Likes to throw his weight. At me. While he bevvies himself senseless. And remember Snapper? The bow-bow? I'm not kidding – he's meaner than Nott. Bit my leg to the bone yesterday. Not pretty!

So listen, Mols, there's no way Mum can ever come near this place but can you just tell her and Dad I'm Calm enough but want home. I can't get near Nott's phone – anyway all the lines are still screwed, aren't they? – because I don't sleep in the farmhouse. Was I meant to? Don't know if I'd want to. It's manky. My digs are Nott's barn. With the pigs. Told Mum my mouldy old dosser coat was a good buy! Though I could do with a sleeping bag. And a pillow. And . . .

Air-freshener

cheese

sugar

tea

kettle

socks

a washing machine

a power-shower

my drumkit

a radiator . . .

Hint hint. Still, your boyfriend's a good guy who feeds me if he can and I've running water (i.e. a dripping tap). That's more than Mum and Dad'll have back home unless the reservoir's decontaminated, yeah? For scran I'm living on all the baked beans (toot toot) Mum made me lug down here – thank you, Mum! Sorry I gave you grief about the weight of them – plus bread swiped from the bashed loaves Nott buys to feed the pigs. This lorryload gets dumped every day and I pick out a loaf before the pigs dig in or before it lands in the slurry. LOOXURY!

Gotta go, but listen, gotta get out to see you guys soon. Either that or I go AWOL.

Love love love. Get me outa here!!!

J

Imagine feeling trainsick in First Class? What a waste! Well I do. As sick now, reclining in my big comfy seat as I did when I read John's letter. What he told me. What he asked me.

Pernilla frowns, 'You OK, Molly? You've turned pale.'

I can only nod and try not to gag when I recall how I shredded John's letter then flushed it away and ignored Fergal who was waiting outside the toilets to tell me he personally witnessed Grumpy Nott scudding John across the head, then slamming him against a wall . .

You see, I've decided I better keep all of this Naughty Nott stuff a secret from Mum and my Dad. When they ask how John's doing I'll just need to tell them what John said in his letter: John's 'Calm', I'll report. A bit too far away from Pernilla's and too busy working for me to visit. But the good news, I'll tell Mum and my Dad, is that my pal Fergal lives near John. He keeps me up to date on what John's up to.

And Fergal says John's OK, I'll tell Mum and my Dad. I'll lie.

Well, what options do I have? If Mum and my Dad learn how rough things are for John they'll make him come back to Glasgow. He'll end up drafted into ForcesUK.

And if John goes home, I'll have to come home too. Just as I'm settling in.

And I don't want to leave Paradise Farm, I decide, as the train approaches Glasgow.

Not yet. I'd miss Pernilla too much.

And Phil . . .

And OK. I'd miss Fergal Lyons too. As a *friend*, of course.

15
Dirty Old Town

This sounds spammy, but I must be so used to tall, slim, graceful Pernilla that when I first see Mum I'm surprised how wide and round and dumpy she seems blarging her way up the platform at Queen Street Station on her swollen lankles (that's what us Fogarty's call ankles as thick as legs). The arms of her old shiny black Just For Walking You To School, Molly, Not For Strutting The Catwalk anorak, or jaisket as she calls it, are waving like inflatable windsocks. And my Dad, he's belting behind Mum, carrying her handbag and his raincoat's flapping and his wee tea biscuit bald spot's shining beneath the station lights and all the heads are flying off the bunch of flowers he's holding.

'Molly!' he's shouting.

'Molly!' Mum's shouting loud enough to drown out

the tannoy announcement about reporting anyone in the station behaving abnormally.

So can you guess the first thing I think as Mum's crushing me half to death in her arms and my Dad's crushing both of us in his and his hand's stroking my hair and he's saying over and over, 'Look at you! Glowing, Molly! Isn't she, Kitty?'

Well, I think lots of things, actually:

Mum, why the heck are you wearing your horrible bobbly old house-skirt to meet me?

And why's your hair gone mad?

What's Pernilla going to make of you?

I also think. *I'm* horrible. What does it matter how Mum looks. It's just so peachy to see her and my Dad. Even though it *hurts*. That's the next thing I think because this missing Mum and my Dad feeling *mushrooms* inside me like a bomb-cloud rising. It chokes me. Fills my eyes with tears. Gives me this *pain*. Deep and twisty and tuggy.

And either your raincoat's too big, or you're shrinking and you face is all shilpit like you're not eating properly, I think about my Dad though I can't speak because my throat's tight from looking at him.

Then I realise I'm being rude because Pernilla's here and I haven't introduced her so I break away from Mum and turn round to pull Pernilla over to join us. Then I think, *Whoah. That's weird.*

Because Pernilla keeps her distance and doesn't take the hand Mum offers and when Mum tries a hug instead – 'Hel-*lo* Pernilla, so lovely to meet you at last. I'm Kitty. This is Denis. Welcome . . .' – Pernilla folds her arms till Mum steps back.

'Mrs Fogarty. Mr Fogarty. Pleased to meet you.' Pernilla stands very stiff and straight, same as when she takes assembly and she's waiting for silence. She greets Mum and my Dad with a tilt of her long neck. She doesn't smile. Her reaction puts Mum in a flap.

'Is everything all right? Is Molly behaving or – You been a good girl? You're all dressed up in new clothes. What's the story with these army trousers?'

'Molly's perfect. A delight, Mrs Fogarty. A credit to you,' Pernilla cuts in. She's giving Mum the frown she usually saves for Fergal. 'Apart from her appalling concentration in class. I don't know *what* kind of education Molly's had in Glasgow, but she is *dreadfully* behind –'

And it's all your fault, Mrs F. Even a R-e-l-u-c-t-a-n-t L-e-a-r-n-e-r like myself catches the accusation in Pernilla's head toss.

'We'd to revise *times tables*.' Pernilla's frizzle quivers. 'And as for spelling –'

'And that's all that's wrong? Thought you'd joined the Forces, or something.' Mum tries to muster a disappointed-in-me face, but it dilutes into her smile at seeing me back.

'How's my darlin'? Have you made friends? And listen, how's John? We've had no word, and no address, and I've posted notes to you to pass on but they can't have arrived because I've never heard back from either of you. Anyway, we're missing you both so much. Aren't we, Denis? You take Pernilla's bag and we'll get off to the bus stop . . .'

I'm off the hook about John for now because words spill out like Mum's been storing them up and she doesn't stop long enough to hear anything I say. Her arm's round my waist as we walk up the platform so I put mine through hers. I must be growing taller because my hip fits the cushioned curve of hers and we lock together.

'It's brilliant. Didn't you get my letter about the farm?' I ask Mum as we head out the station and I finally get a word in. I pick my topic carefully. 'Except school. It's boring,' I whisper. 'She's a strict teacher,' I whisper, because Pernilla's right behind me.

'I bet she is. And nearly as thin and gorgeous as myself,' Mum chuckles and tickles my side. 'Coming up here for the weekend must be a shock to your system, Pernilla.' Mum camouflages my splutter by calling over her shoulder.

'Oh, I'm used to bigger cities than Glasgow. I've lived in New York and I'm from London of course, so I think I'll survive,' Pernilla clips back at Mum.

Whoah! Is she eating her words when the four of us step from the station into the epicentre of a Strike Zone. Or 'a spot of trouble' as my Dad describes the situation we're in when Mum grabs him round the neck and asks, 'Lord, what's happening now, Denis?'

Not that he could answer her any more accurately.

God knows what's going on but the centre of Glasgow's in chaos: sirens yowling, buildings burning, people screaming, shouting, running . . .

'This can't be real,' Pernilla gasps.

'I know,' I whisper, feeling like a Final Level Target in a 18+ Explicit Violence Certificate game John's not supposed to let me play: *Ultimate Carnage, Uber Decimation* . . .

Because *this* is the first time The Emergency's really come close. I mean, I've lost count how often I've had to run to a shelter, for drills mainly, and I've heard explosions in the distance, and I know people who know people who've been toxed – but *this* is here. So in my face I *have* to record a Wide-Sweep vid-text with sound.

Oh!!! George Sqre Burning. Have 2 go 2 Undrgrnd.

I stop to caption the film I'll show Fergal on Monday, even though I bet he'll think it's sick.

My Dad doesn't appreciate what I'm doing either.

'Keep moving, Molly!'

Searching out a Safe Bunker, he's running Pernilla and me and Mum – well, more sort of hauling Mum on her puffy lankles. She's stumbling after us all, tripping and panting. And ALL The Emergency warning sirens are screeching at once:

Waooooo. Eeeeeee. Tratratratratraaaaaa Yayayayaya.
GasMissileBombDANGERTake Shelter . . .

'I'd no idea you lived like this, Molly. Hell,' Pernilla gasps. And gasps. And gasps. She can say that again because the first night of my first night home for yonks, we don't even get home! Thanks very much, Mr Suicide Bomber who hijacked a Glasgow City Tour bus full of foreign students. Then drove it into the Gulf War Memorial. Boom!

So me and Pernilla and Mum and my Dad have to sleep – well, we don't sleep – we slump against sweaty tiles in the ex-Buchanan Street Underground Station. No food. Water. Toilets. A crossed-leg crisis situation, Mum calls it.

'More like a *nightmare!*' Pernilla gasps as she smoothes out the plastic bag Mum's given her to sit on. 'How can you be so relaxed about everything? It's filthy and smelly and dark and dangerous.'

Pernilla's too uptight and upset to enjoy the free Underground entertainment that almost takes my mind off the crumps and explosions overhead. She clutches her handbag to her chest like it's her teddy, and doesn't laugh once at all the stotious Friday-night clubbers who pour from the pubs into our shelter when the alerts go off. Not even when the communal singing starts, and me and Mum join in with this half-cut girl on the other side of the Underground platform, whose spangly boob tube totally falls down when she swings her arms in the air for the final chorus of that 'Angels' tune poor old Robbie Williams used to sing. (I make sure I phone-film all of it so I can trade Fergal for a report about John.) Everyone except Pernilla keeps cheering her to do it again, and she does, till a mental fight breaks out between a bunch of bampots with knives.

'Don't listen.' Mum covers my ears with her hands.

'Don't look.' My Dad covers me with his raincoat, but not before a skinhead guy is slashed across the face and I see it all.

'I don't believe you can expose Molly to this. Is there nothing we can do to keep her safe?' Pernilla presses Mum and my Dad till they gather up and hustle me to a quieter part of the Underground where everyone, apart from us Fogartys and Pernilla, is heavy snogging. And the rest.

'All sort of jiggery-pokery, eh, Kitty?'

'Obscene,' clips Pernilla.

'Like there's no tomorrow. Don't blame them. What a world for the young,' my Dad mutters to Mum.

Who keeps tugging my head on to her lap.

'You try and rest now, Molly.'

No chance. I'm Eyes Wide Open, drinking in the Dos and Don'ts of Kissing. Well, it kind of takes my mind off the sirens, still howling above. The muffled explosions rocking the Underground, shaking the grout from the tiles.

When I'm out the tunnel. *If* I get out the tunnel, I can practise what I learn on my pillow.

Just in case I *have* to snog someone in the near future. You never know . . .

16

The Long Walk Home

It's late mid-morning before the All Clear drills. Finally we're Identichecked (Much to Pernilla's disgust: 'This has *never* happened to me before. Do I look like a terrorist?') then allowed to straggle up the down escalators with all the other Underground dwellers.

'Eventually, eh Molly?' Mum pants at my side. 'You all right there, Pernilla?'

'Fantastic, Mrs Fogarty,' says Pernilla. She doesn't sound it.

Probably she's hungry. Same as me. Thirsty. Cramped. Longing for a Pernilla-bubble soak and a change of clothes . . .

'Come on! Starving!' I try to gee Mum up, remembering the dozen eggs Phil gave me to give Mum because I told him how she misses eggs more than any food that's rationed. I fancy dipping buttered soldiers in one of them. Soft boiled. Soft bread.

I tug on Mum's hand as we stumble into daylight. Instead of keeping up with me though, she freezes.

'Oh, in the name of God.'

She's gawping at a giant crater blasted into the ground where George Square used to be. There's nothing but a hole. No statues. No pigeons. No drunks necking Special Brew. Just a gouge in the middle of Glasgow cordoned off with tatty red police tape.

'Come on, girls. Home.' My Dad marches Mum and me and Pernilla from the bombsite. He even snatches the phone out my hand while I'm filming and text-captioning:

Glasgow City Chmbrs. All wndws smsh . . .

'Molly. Show respect.'

'But Dad, I just wanna show my pal Fergal . . .'

I'm thinking it's unfair of my Dad to speak to me in his angry-with-John voice.

Pernilla's sweeping *her* phone across over the bombsite, and he doesn't say anything.

He doesn't chib Mum either even though she's walking backwards, pausing every two minutes to sigh and do a spammy-mammy. I mean, it's thanks to her, as much as the suicide bomber who stopped all the buses running, that it takes us two and a half hours to schlep home.

Mum hardly speaks the whole way. Well, she can't because her lips are pressed together like they're superglued. They always do that when her lankles squelch out over her shoes. She lurches beside my Dad. Soooo sloooow. 'Specially compared to Pernilla's power-walk pace. It's actually less tiring to keep up with Pernilla than to straggle with Mum, so the two of us set off striding ahead till I notice Mum and my Dad are miles behind us. We slow down, wait for Mum to catch up.

'Sorry, sorry, girls. I'm ancient, fat and slow,' she smiles before we tear off again. Only to double back a few blocks later and hear Mum pant her apology once more.

'It's like we're attached to one of those bungee-run elastics that wheech you back to where you started,' I giggle at Pernilla after we've shuttled back to the slowcoaches once too often for her liking. That's what I'm guessing since I've just heard her tut and mutter, 'What the hell am I doing here?'

I don't feel right admitting this, but Pernilla being annoyed makes *me* feel annoyed. With Mum. Annoyed that she's fat. Impatient that she's shambling behind, embarrassing me with her puffy legs and her shabby, unpulse clothes and her mad grey hair.

'Hurry up, Mum, will you? We're never going to get home. Only here one more night,' I tut too. *You're a state*, I'm about to add but my Dad speaks sharply.

'Mum's doing her best. You just look out for a taxi and a butcher's.'

Taxi? There's more chance I'll see Elvis jiving up the street! There's so little traffic – just army patrols, tox-mask wardens – I could back-flip down the middle of the road if I wasn't so hungry and tired and scunnered off. We don't pass any butcher's either. Most food shops are shut, some of them for good. Any open display

117

VOUCHER ONLY notices in the window. None of them sells milk.

Milk! I can blooming bathe in the stuff at Pernilla's . . .

17

Slumming It

'Pity about the milk,' my Dad sighs, unlocking our front door at last. 'You'll have to slum it with powdered, girls. And I fancied doing a fry-up: sausages, bacon, potato-scones. Still,' his smile's hungry as he gestures Pernilla into our hallway first, 'what about those lovely eggs from your husband?'

What about those eggs? Two dozen. Extra, extra large. Free range.

'Musta had one of my oopsidents on the way home. I'm that clumsy . . .' is Mum's explanation for why they end up as a yolky puddle at the bottom of one of her shoppers.

So, forget eggy soldiers (Pernilla's are soooo peachy). We've to slum it on tinned, over the sell-by date pineapples and stale Ryvita. Yesterday I was noshing fluffy pancakes with cream and homemade raspberry jam for brekkie. Hot chocolate! Today in Good Old Glasgow I drink tea with powdered milk floaters and Pernilla goes without her skinny latte. Goes without her breakfast altogether, actually. First time she's ever done that since I've known her.

'I'm off my food,' she says.

And as for that Pernilla-scented bubble bath . . .

There's no running water.

All weekend!!!

Don't think Pernilla's too impressed. No. Despite her clapping her hands together and giggling a lot at me or saying things to Mum like, 'Oooh, this flat's so terribly *cosy*. Takes me right back to my student digs in East London. Four of us sharing one bathroom. And (Pernilla's squealing here) I don't believe this – *we'd* a big leather settee with patches on the arms just like your suite. And almost those same beige curtains. I can see you're all still into that distressed look. I'd a phase of that myself about ten years ago . . .'

I've a deep-down feeling that Pernilla's deep-down thinking how us Fogartys live our lives is crap, basically. And despite Pernilla insisting, 'Listen. The Emergency's hardly *your* fault, Mrs Fogarty. I'm just *fine*,' when Mum apologises yet again for the lack of heat or decent food or water on tap, I'm sure Pernilla's fibbing beneath her smile.

In fact, when Mum tells me, 'How about you show Pernilla to the guest room?' I'm left in no doubt what Pernilla thinks about our set-up in Glasgow.

Because while I'm giggling, 'Mum's kidding on she's posh. We don't have a spare room. She means John's tip,' Pernilla grabs my hand and whispers, 'Seeing you live like this kills me, sweetheart. No fresh food. No power. No heating. Everything dark and drab. Everyone just making do.'

I'm still giggling, hoping I can make Pernilla giggle too as I open the door on a space that's ninety-five per cent drumkit, five per cent bed. *But empty-looking all the same*, I gulp, without John to crash about in it. And – brrrr – much colder than the rest of the flat. Which is saying something!

When Pernilla steps into John's room she doesn't even pretend she doesn't like what she sees. 'Someone actually *sleeps* in here? But the paper's torn off the walls and they're damp patches behind the bed –'

'Yeah. Our water tank's on the roof and a mortar or something burst a hole in it last year so water was leaking right down, through all the flats in the close, and nobody knew till paper started peeling off everyone's wall like this –'

'And your Mum left the room in this state? Without redecorating? And she sleeps her son in here? Guests?' Pernilla doesn't seem keen to put her bag down anywhere. She keeps it hovering above John's bed while she glares round his tatty walls, like all the lairy guys in his music posters have mooned her.

'How can you exist like this? It's third world Armageddon.'

'John likes it. Thinks it's punk. I quite like it too –'

'Not just *this*.'

Pernilla sweeps her hand from John's bed to the window like she wants to deck everything away. Since it would be ultra-rude to slag someone's décor, I take it she must be meaning Partick, the part of Glasgow where our flat is. Or, maybe just Glasgow in general.

I shrug. 'Yeah. The Emergency's a total *pain* but you just have to kid on everything's normal. That's what Mum says.'

'Does she? This is normal? Well, I think it's hell. And the sooner you and I get home to Phil . . .' Pernilla hisses just as Mum pops her head round the door.

'Comfy, Pernilla? Anything you need? Cuppa tea? Slica crispbread?'

'Nothing, Mrs Fogarty. Everything's wonderful. I'm just going to get settled and take a nap –'

'Sure you don't need anything? Extra blankets? One of my cardies in case you're cold?'

'I'm *perfect*, Mrs Fogarty.' Pernilla puts her hand on John's door handle. Mum doesn't take the hint. She comes further into the room and sinks down on the bed.

'Listen. I didn't get the story about John yet.' Because Mum rubs her hand on John's old Narnia stickers when she speaks, and doesn't look up, I can't tell if her remark is to me or Pernilla. That's why I say nothing. Let Pernilla handle this.

'Oh, he's excellent, I believe. Working hard, of

course.' Pernilla answers vaguely because she's delving about in her handbag.

'Hang on. You say you "believe"? So you haven't seen John? All these weeks?' Mum's left hand covers the Narnia stickers on the headboard like she's protecting them, the other creeping to her chest. She's looking from me to Pernilla, her face crumpling.

'The ironic thing is, Mrs Fogarty, I'd actually planned to pop in on your son this weekend . . . Remember I suggested it, Molly?' Pernilla taps me with the toilet bag she's holding.

Did you? I rack my brains to recall something I swear I never heard Pernilla discuss with me.

'But never mind,' she sing-songs. 'There's next weekend, eh?' She leans towards me to stage whisper behind her hand, 'That's if we manage to get out of Glasgow alive –'

'Another week and no news.' Mum's easing herself off John's bed. First she nods, then she shakes her head. 'That's no use at all,' she sighs, smoothing away the sump her bum's made on John's duvet.

Something in her tone seems to worry Pernilla.

'Listen. If you're really desperate for news, Mrs Fogarty, I'll find out on Monday. Can send you a telegram. Put your mind at ease –'

Mum attends to John's bed instead of answering. When she does speak, it's to me, not to Pernilla.

'I think your Dad and me'll need to be getting John home if nobody goes to see how he's doing. You'd need to come home too, darlin'.'

'Not yet,' Pernilla and I chime together, the pair of us suddenly finding ourselves sitting on John's bed side-by-side, pinged together like magnets.

'I promise you son's marvellous where he is. And safe. You mustn't be hasty.' Pernilla stares into Mum's eyes without blinking. I do the same.

'And my friend Fergal from school sees John all the time because he lives near him, and he told me John told him to tell you he's Calm. Dead busy though, so he doesn't get time off,' I gasp.

And what I tell Mum's true, isn't it? Every careful word.

Still, to avoid more questions from Mum, who's looking into my eyes like she can read my mind, I give her a massive yawn and do a Pernilla and take to my bed even though it's only the afternoon. There I lie, glum as a drill-session in a school safe bunker, wishing I was back at Paradise Farm. Clean. Well-fed. Warm. Because it's blinking cold, even after Mum comes in to check on me and throws extra covers over my own and shuts the window behind the blackout screen.

'I've bad vibes about John, darlin'. Me and your Dad are through in the kitchen talking about things down by –' Mum kisses me absent-mindedly, bustling from the room already.

'What things?' I call after her, but she doesn't wait to answer.

At the mouth of our close, posh Patsy's voice tannoys from a Curfew truck: *Clea the streets. Clea the streets* . . . while from my bed I strain to listen in to the chat Mum and my Dad are having through the wall:

'Denis, I wish John . . . home. There's something Molly's not . . . and I know Pernilla thinks I'm just some old . . .'

'. . . but we know Molly's safer there, Kitty, John

too . . . and Molly's just . . . look at her . . . she's better than . . .'

'Oh, I can see . . . thriving . . . you're right . . . wants for nothing . . . Wee edge to her . . . didn't have three weeks ago . . .'

'. . . Kitty . . . be like that wherever . . . nearly a teenage girl . . .'

'. . . but not like my Molly when she give me that . . . but I'm grateful she's . . . and so well cared for . . . and a bit of schooling, but Denis . . . John . . . I'm that worried . . .'

I struggle to stay awake, but after a sleepless night Mum and my Dad's voices and the familiar chink and clink of cutlery and crockery and pots and pans drug me like a lullaby. I bob from my bunk on the rise and fall of their chat, drifting to a wishful sleep in my other bedroom. Purplicious. Shimmery.

And, *'Hey, Mum, Listen!'* I try to shout. John's nearby because I can hear him: *'Check this out, Mols,'* he's saying, showing me where he's been bitten on the leg by evil Farmer Nott's dog. *'Just because I asked to go home to Glasgow . . .*

'. . . *But I'm Calm. Tell everyone I'm Calm, Molly, or I'll be doing a drum roll on your head . . .*' the John of my nap threatens.

So I try to make my mouth mumble, 'John's *fine*, Mum. Hear what he's telling you? So please. I don't need to leave Pernilla's yet . . .'

But I'm paralysed by sleep and my words won't form. Anyway, Mum isn't listening.

She's too busy worrying: 'Denis, I don't know if we're doing the right thing.'

'Denis, maybe it would be better if Molly and John just came back home.'

Shut up. Shut up. Shut up. My little snide head-voice pipes up to silence Mum. *Why would I want to come home yet just because of John? I'm having a ball. Can't you see everything's way peachier at Pernilla's than it is here?*

18

Dinner is Served #2

'Dinnah is served,' Mum announces from the hall while my Dad clicks two of John's drumsticks together and toots a fanfare. This is all in honour of the bowls of soup sitting at three of the four places round our kitchen table.

'Eight shops before I found tomato. Only one on the shelf, like it had our name on it,' my Dad tells me, rubbing his hands together and drinking in the steam in front of him. 'Haven't seen tinned tomato soup for weeks, only that powdered muck.'

'Snap. Neither has Molly,' Pernilla smiles at him.

'Well. Here's a treat. Your favourite, darlin',' Mum says, busy stirring something on the camping stove. 'And just you all start. I'll skip to the main course.'

'Why's that, Mum?' I'm already digging in, same

as my Dad, though to be honest, the soup's thin, like Mum's watered it down. Or maybe I've just grown used to the homemade flavours of the fresh vegetable soups Pernilla cooks. A different one every day, *her* tomato soup perfumed with basil and so thick even Mum could stomp across a plate of it without sinking.

As I shove my bowl away, unfinished, I notice Pernilla's soup's untouched. She's sitting up straight in her chair, hands in her lap, watching Mum.

'Are you on a diet, Mrs Fogarty? Or can't you eat this kind of food, either, because I'm afraid I can't.'

'Oh. You don't like –' Mum lifts Pernilla's soup away from the table then comes back with it. Tips it all into my Dad's empty bowl.

'Oi, what about you, Kitty? You thought there wasn't enough to go –'

'Go ahead. Eat up before it's cold,' Mum cuts in, 'and I'm sorry Pernilla. I never thought –'

'Not your fault.' Pernilla beams Mum a really kind smile. 'I just can't put processed food inside me. Frankly, I'd rather go without.'

'Well, we've no choice,' I hear Mum sigh.

Over at the cooker she's dishing up corned-beef stovies, the potatoes like wallpaper paste out a packet because my Dad couldn't find fresh spuds anywhere. The mushy peas to go with them splot from yet another tin.

'Listen, don't bother about feeding me, Mrs Fogarty. It's time I had a de-tox fast anyway. Have you ever tried that yourself?' Pernilla crosses her hands over her place when Mum tries to serve her.

'Only when there's been no food in the shops. Anyway,' Mum chuckles as she sits down and tucks into her stovies, 'supermodels like myself don't have to fast, do they, Molly?'

Pernilla definitely can't have the same sense of humour as us Fogartys, because she doesn't burst out laughing like me and my Dad as we watch Mum shoving three big forkfuls into her face one after another so her cheeks are bursting when she grins round the table and splutters, 'My body is a temple.'

'Actually,' Serious, like she's going to talk about my schoolwork, Pernilla changes the subject, 'speaking of bodies, I must tell you how fantastically athletic this girl of ours is. She's limber as a monkey.'

Huh? I'm frowning at Pernilla because what she's said is *so* not true. 'Utterly inflexible in mind and body,' Squishbutt wrote in my last St Peter's report card. She was dead right. Honestly, I think Pernilla reads me all wrong sometimes. Believes I smirk in class because I'm *sweet*. Mind you her *monkey* comparison's spot on. I was being a cheeky one all through the gym period she's telling Mum and my Dad about.

What happened was that instead of climbing non-stop up and down the wallbars while she supervised bean-bag hopping races with the Frizzle girls, I was dreeping upside down. No hands. Fergal beside me. We were competing to see who could stand our eyes bloobing and the blood rushing up to our heads the longest without going dizzy (my idea) till Pernilla heard Fergal yelling, 'Paws off, Foghorn!' (I'd nipple-grippled him.) *He* was sent off to the changing room for Arrant Boldness while Pernilla made all the Frizzle girls bunny-hop over to admire my dangling skills.

'Yes, Molly's *so* flexible,' Pernilla takes my hand

132

across the table.

'Is she? Must take after her old mother,' Mum snorts, helping herself to mushy peas from my plate.

'Actually it's not a joke, Mrs Fogarty. If Molly was mine I'd be so proud of her talent. Look into sending her to gymnastics. I'd make sure she can be all she can be.' Pernilla's finished talking but her eyes fix on Mum. Even in candlelight they've turned beady, and while Pernilla holds her stare this *silence* freezes the room. No one moves and I daren't turn my head in case Pernilla snaps at me next, though I don't need to look at Mum to know she's lost by what's been said. She never argues with anyone. Hates upsetting people . . .

'Kitty, that athletic gene definitely comes from you,' my Dad chuckles, patting Mum's hand. 'You're always thinking about getting fit. Remember a few years back when you heard jogging was the most popular sport for women in Scotland. "Anyone can do it, any age, any size" you told me. Bought all the gear –'

'The shoes and headband and gizmo to measure

how many steps you take –' Mum's recovered. Totally, since she can barely get her words out for laughing at herself. 'And out I zip and by the time I get down our hill my lankles are up like balloons and I can't breathe and I'm holding on to my big triple 38G-cups because they're bouncing up and down like they want to run away –'

'And I'm out looking for you in the car because you're too whacked to walk home yourself', my Dad cuts in.

'And that's when I thought: me and exercise – not a good combination.'

Pernilla has to wait for a break in Mum and my Dad's laughter before she can suggest: 'Listen, I'm sure you'd be eligible for breast reduction if that's what's stopping you from keeping fit.' And she's *still* totally serious because she adds, 'It's your duty to stay healthy for Molly's sake. I do weights and yoga and pilates and –'

'Och, no wonder you're so thin and pale,' Mum sighs sympathetically as she licks her fork clean. 'Anyway, there's bigger things in the world to bother about these days than my lumps and bumps.'

My Dad nods along with Mum. His finger and thumb chucks Mum's chin.

'*My* lumps and bumps, Kitty,' he says in his shy voice.

'I don't agree, Mrs Fogarty.' Pernilla rolls her eyes. Then she claps her hands. 'Why don't I give you some exercises you can do in the house? Tonight.'

'Tonight?' Suddenly Mum looks likes she needs her inhaler and I expect that's why she tells such a *giant* whopper.

'Oh, I don't fancy that sort of exercise,' Mum beams at Pernilla, 'but I'm *very* keen on swimming.'

Hel-lo, I'm trying to catch Mum's eye to glare and at the same time stop my jaw from clacking off the table. Er, Mum you *can't* swim. Used to sit in the cafeteria. Eating doughnuts. Watching me.

'But I've had to give up since the water poisoning closed all the Glasgow pools,' Mum lies. 'Our favourite sport, wasn't it, Molly? You miss it *so* much.'

At least Mum and dinner finishes off with the truth.

19

The New Religion

'Listen, Molly, how d'you fancy a treat after our horrible night in the Underground?' This is more confusing than Mum fibbing last night. Here's Pernilla in her swishy purple silk shaking me awake like it's a school day on Paradise Farm. But it's Sunday morning; usually the only day of the week she doesn't rise and shine with the birds.

'Treat? Peachy! All of us?' I grope for my covers and mumble.

'Shh. Just us girlies.'

'You, me and Mum?'

'No, silly. Us *girlies*. We can catch a really early train back to Carlisle instead of waiting here all morning? Spot of lunch somewhere yummy. Shopping this afternoon?'

I don't think I've ever talked or woken up so fast at this hour in the morning. 'Mum, guess what me and Pernilla are doing on the way home? Stopping off to shop in Carlisle. Shops are meant to be totally peachy there.' I burst into the kitchen where Mum's in her pulley-rope dressing gown trying to light the camping stove.

'But I thought we'd have the afternoon together,' she says when I tell her about Pernilla's plans. 'And, before you go anywhere you'll come to church with me and your Dad.'

'But Pernilla doesn't go to church. And she never makes me. And we can't go out and leave her here alone, either. She's our guest. That's so rude –'

My volume level brings both my Dad and Pernilla into the kitchen.

'Everything all right?' Pernilla asks in her brightest voice.

'She doesn't want to leave you in the house by yourself –' Mum begins to explain, but my Dad doesn't let her finish.

'Pernilla can survive without you for an hour. Get yourself dressed, Molly,' he tells me in his lowest voice.

So I do what I'm told though I winge non-stop at

Mum while we hurry, late as usual, down our hill to the church.

'Why do I need to go to Mass today? Pernilla would never make me go –'

'Molly, I don't like the way you're talking,' Mum gasps, shuffling into a pew. Hand to her chest, she squints at me like she doesn't know me.

'Molly,' my Dad leans across Mum to press his finger to my lips. *You've said enough*. But I won't shut up.

'Pernilla thinks it's a waste of time going to church. She says if you're the type of person who believes in God you should be able to pray anywhere coz you believe God's everywhere. If you hadn't dragged me here I'd've prayed on the train for you –'

'Molly!'

Mum has to grip my wrist to silence me.

'What's got into you?' she whispers.

Good question. I've *never* cheeked Mum like this before. During the sermon she shreds a tissue between her fingers, but doesn't actually speak to me again till the collection plate rattles up and down the pews.

'Of course you pray anywhere but as long as you're

with me and your Dad on Sundays we come to Mass
and –'

La La La.

I slither away from Mum so the spit from her holy
whispering doesn't hit my ear. I pick off the yellow nail
varnish Pernilla bought me last Sunday while I tot up
all the tops, shoes, bags, trousers and make-up she's
treated me to so far. Drawing up my list fair makes
Mass skip along briskly. Still, I make sure my face is
tripping me as I leave the church. There's a bottleneck
at the doors, all these people queuing up to light
candles for their dead and missing.

'You'd think religion's the new religion thanks to
The Emergency, wouldn't you, Denis? Will I light one
for our John?' Mum stops in the aisle but I hustle her
onwards and outwards.

'He's not dead or missing, is he? He's *fine* and the
sooner you let me get back to Pernilla's the sooner I'll
check for you. So can I go now?' I yawn and while
Mum huffs and puffs her way up our hill, arm and arm
with my Dad, I march on to the top without them.

*

'Right then, I'm all set and I've packed your bag. Top Shop here we coooome!' Pernilla shucks on her coat as soon as I open the front door. Together, arm in arm, we race back down our hill.

'Your Mum seems older than I imagined. Must be the way she walks,' Pernilla whispers as we hurtle towards Mum and my Dad, still only half way up.

'Mrs Fogarty, you've been wonderful,' Pernilla air-kisses Mum's cheeks.

'You're going already? I've a tin of soup for your lunch –'

'Oh, we'll grab a bite in Edinburgh,' Pernilla's shaking my Dad's hand. 'Should dash though. Think there's a train a train due. So toodleoo, you two.'

'But there's a train later.' Mum tugs the wrist of my hand that's not hooked through Pernilla's. 'When will I see you, darlin'? Feels we've hardly had time to –'

'Kitty, she'll pass our love to John, so we'll let her get off. Missing you already, Molly.' My Dad lays his hand against my cheek. Looks very straight and deep into my eyes. He's smiling and frowning at the same time.

'I'll come back in a couple of weeks,' I gulp. Peck him.

'Promise.' I look into Mum's eyes.

I lie.

Then Pernilla yanks my arm from Mum's grip and we hurry away.

'Ohh. That's better. Spot of retail therapy and I feel myself again. How about you?' Pernilla beams at me over a mountain of shopping bags when we're back in First Class.

'You OK, Molly? You're quiet. Tired out? You look tired. And hungry. And I bet you're desperate for a hot bath. Don't worry, Phil knows to meet the train and take us home. I told him we'd be early.'

Home.

Hmmmm . . .

I pluck at the bags and parcels on the seat beside me. Another pair of winter boots, another peachy jacket, fluffy cushions to match my purplicious walls. Honestly, I'm as confused at the end of this day as I was at the beginning.

'I don't know where home is any more,' I blurt before I can stop myself. Must be tired right enough because my voice doesn't know whether to laugh or cry. As soon as the words are said I see Mum's face in my mind's eye.

'What would Mum say if she heard me?' I slap my hand to my mouth. *And I never said sorry to her for my cheek in church. We hardly spoke. All weekend. And I couldn't wait to rush away. To go shopping.*

Thinking about Mum and my Dad is giving me an ache inside my chest, under my ribs. Feels like my heart's trying to escape and reach all the way back ho–

Except . . .

I don't know where home is any more. The ache in my ribcage grows so sharp I gasp when Pernilla clutches me to her.

'If you feel Paradise Farm's like home then you've just paid me the biggest compliment ever, Molly. Made me feel like your Mum,' she kisses me. And kisses me. And tickles me till I'm begging her to stop and the picture of Mum's face in my head fades with the miles.

20
Temptation

And you know that saying: Time passes quickly when you're having fun. Well, take it from me: it's true.

Pernilla and I are *soooo* busy we don't once mention my next visit to Glasgow till the postman delivers a telegram through Pernilla's car window as we're leaving Paradise Farm for school three Fridays after my last visit.

'Ooops. We've been naughty girls. You should have gone to Glasgow last weekend. Listen to this:

3 WEEKS +. NO VISIT. IS ALL WELL? NO
WORD JOHN? COME FRIDAY. FOUR NIGHTS.
MUM. DAD.'

Pernilla turns into a Dalek, complete with swivel

143

and pointing arm. While she's driving, by the way.
Mum would freak.

'Oh dear, what's our excuse, Molly?' Pernilla
goes back to Dalek-speak.

'SCHOOL. SHOPPING. COOKING. HAVING THE
TIME OF OUR LIVES. EATING PROPERLY.
TAKING BUBBLE BATHS.
NOT GETTING KILLED.

That'll be one expensive reply.'

'Friday's today. I'll need to go.'

'But four whole nights this time. Such a long, long,
long time to be away. I'll so miss my Molly-Wolly,'
Pernilla mumps. Then she grips my hand, serious again.
'And I'll worry sick, Molly, sending you into that grotty
third-world war-zone when you're safe here. Plus,' as
Pernilla takes the speed bump too fast her frizzle quivers
like jelly with a fever, 'you'll miss school on Monday.
And I'm arranging to take the Uppers swimming.'

Er . . . sorry.

'I'll miss swimming?'

'There's a brand-new pool in Selkirk. Was keeping it as a surprise for this weekend. I think I'll try it out myself if you're away . . .' Pernilla taps the steering wheel, humming to a tune on the radio.

'All that swimming chat with your Mum put me in the mood,' she goes on. 'What a *shame* you can't come with me. *La la la . . .'*

Fields pass. Pernilla overtakes the school bus on a corner. It's not until we drive into the schoolyard that she suggests what I'm biting my tongue not to suggest myself . . . 'You know, I'm just wondering if your Mum would mind so *terribly* if I kept you here this weekend. Your Mum and Dad have given such short notice.' Pernilla cuts the engine. 'And I've plans for you. Like an appointment to do something different with *this.*' Pernilla curls a strand of my hair round her finger and whispers, her eyes glittery.

'I can send her a telegram at lunchtime. Say you want to stay here.'

'Peachy,' I nod.

Of course I do.

And to make myself stop imagining the expression

I know Mum's face'll wear when she reads the telegram, I force myself to stare straight across the yard at Fergal waving till I'm close enough to count his freckles.

'Hey, Foghorn, *finally* you can't take your eyes off me. Sorry, I'm just too buff,' Fergal pouts at me while Pernilla flaps him aside to pass into school.

'Delivery,' Fergal grabs my hand as I follow Pernilla.

When I slip into the girls' toilets to recover from the shock of his touch I'm holding a scrap of scribbled-on newspaper.

Hey Mols,
How come Ferg says you've not been back to see Mum and Dad for weeks? I'd give anything to be home in Glasgow! And on the subject, still no word about me getting OUTA HERE!!!
Please.
Do something.
Come see me at least!!
I can't stay with alcho-Nott much longer.

John, reporting for duty. Hint hint.
xxxxx
P.S. I picked up a ForcesUK recruitment leaflet in Galashiels. Pay's good. Hint hint hint . . .

'Well, Foghorn?' Fergal has the nerve to poke his curls round the toilet door while I'm still reading.

'Well, what? You being a perv, peering into the girls' lav. There's no snog for this note if that's what you're after –'

'Dream on, Foghorn.' Fergal's actually sneering. 'Just want to check you read your note then *do* something about it instead of kidding on you belong to Miss –'

'Fergal Lyons. Why on earth are you in the girls' lavatory?'

Pernilla frogmarches Fergal up the corridor to the Headmaster before I tell him we'll probably never meet again if I show Mum or my Dad the note I've just flushed. I don't see him for the rest of school. Pity that, because Pernilla's decided to give us a fun day.

There are no sums or interpretations for once. Just drawing ponies and ballerinas for the Frizzle girls. Uninterrupted dead-mouse spinning for the runny-nose boys and non-educational DVDs for me. Peachiest of all, there's no homework for *anyone* in Uppers.

'All in honour of you staying with Nilly when you could have gone to Glasgow,' Pernilla tells me when we leave Valley Juniors at the end of the day. 'I want to make this your Best Weekend Ever,' she promises.

21
Best Weekend Ever

An hour after we leave school me and Pernilla are in a pool and she's splooshing.

Riding the flumes. Holding my hand. Waiting for the wave machine to start.

Squealing louder than me when it does, then beating me into the biggest roller.

She dive-bombs me when I'm not looking.

Grabs my legs underwater and dunks me.

Holds on to the side of the pool and kicks froth in my face till I beg her for mercy.

Honest it's the *best* laugh I've had since . . . ooooh, I can't remember.

This is what dawns on me just after losing my race with Pernilla: I've never *played* with Mum like this. Mum's arthritic not athletic. She gets puffed out *watching* people exercising so *never* could she beat me in an underwater breath-holding contest like Pernilla does. And as for Mum fluming in a rubber doughnut!

'Hey, Molly, so glum. Upset I beat you? Don't be. You'd wipe me in no time if you swam regularly . . .'

Upset? There Pernilla goes again. Reading me *all* wrong. How could she think I'm looking upset when everything we've done since we left school's been perfect? I mean the bell was still ringing and Pernilla has me whisked off in her car to buy . . . OK: my new swimsuit's definitely not from a Tesco's bargain bin like my last one. It's bought from this pulse *boutique*. Looks like it's made of mermaid scales sewn over metal mesh. It has a zigzag zip from shoulder to thigh that reacts with water and glows multi-coloured and it fits me like . . . Look, the best thing about my swimsuit is that it makes me swim *nearly* as fast as Pernilla in her almost identical costume when we race each other.

That's right: her. An adult. Races. With me. A child. For fun.

'I'm not upset.' I shake my head so my hair flicks her face. 'I'm just *really* glad I didn't go home now. This is much more fun. I love it here. Wish I could stay forever. Thankyouthankyouthankyou.' I flop back into the water and clasp Pernilla's shoulders. It doesn't start off as a hug – I'm trying to pull her under – but because she keeps holding me it sort of becomes one. Pernilla's arms round me. Tight. We're twirling a bouncy ring-a-ring o' roses in the water.

'Stay forever?' She hugs tighter. 'You know, Molly. That could be arranged.'

In the excitement of *not* swimming for two years I can't think of *anywhere* I'd rather spend the rest of my life than *here*: this brand-new pool. That's what *I* think Pernilla's talking about . . .

Nothing else.

But you know what? You *can* get too much of a good thing.

You can get too much swimming anyway.

After three splish and flume sessions in one weekend, the novelty wears off. That's why ***GOING SWIMMING*** doesn't even make *Top 3* in my **Peachy Brilliant Top 5 Stuff that Happens with Pernilla**

in the Best Weekend Ever! I text a list into my phone so I'll remember when I tell Adele all about it . . . *if* I get to tell Adele all about it . . .

Anyway, *GOING SWIMMING* is *Number 4*.

At least it's higher than *SEEING JOHN*.

He's bottom, *Number 5* and we meet on the Sunday afternoon of my Best Weekend Ever. By accident.

Nearly *serious* accident because Pernilla's boy-racering a twisty back-road to this farm she wants me to visit.

'We've just *got* to check out something you'll love, Molly,' is all she'll tell me as she puts her foot down, takes a bend, and nearly roadsplats this guy crossing with a plate of food in his hands.

'Moron . . .' Pernilla flats her hand on her horn and accelerates up the verge she's skidding. *Vroooom!*

'Stop,' I scream louder than her wheelspin. 'That's Fergal!'

He's scrambling a stile into an opposite field. His plate's being wheeched out of his hands already by a waiting tramp. A tramp with dyed blond hair.

I do a double take. It's John's ratty coat I recognise

first. Not the skinny stranger with the straggly beard and the black eyes who's wearing it.

'There's John, too. *Please* stop,' I beg Pernilla. Which she does, with a tut. She zigzag reverses, nearly mowing John down this time. He's chasing the car, and when I hear his big voice booming 'Molly!' it actually *hurts* inside my chest. ALL I want to do is escape from Pernilla's car and run to him. Soon as Pernilla slows down enough I'm pelting along the middle of the road.

'John. John. **John!!!**'

Anyone driving past this scene'd swear they were witnessing the reunion of The World's Most Loving Brother and Sister.

But hey, get real.

Any soppy business is Ancient Scottish History as soon as I'm close enough for John to get a good squint at me . . .

Or should I say: for John to get a good squint at me and *Number 2: MY BRAND-NEW FRIZZLE* (which to be honest feels more like planet-sized candy-floss teetering on my head than a pulse hairdo).

And for *me* to get a snifter of him and his cacky clothes.

Phwoah!! John's reeking of . . . I'm guessing sweat and dirt and pigs. Mixed with the fry-up and HP sauce he's scoffing it's not a good combo. But before I can slag him for honking he points a sausage at my hair and brays:

'Check the fuzzball. Molly the ginger GOLLY!' Then he's pressing his hand on the top of my head, going, *'Boinggggee! Boinggggee!* Why d'you stick your fingers in a socket? D'you wanna *die* rather than stay here, too?'

Now, if it was just John on his own, insulting me like this, I'd be Right Back At Him: *Hey, Smelly-keks. At least I don't ming like a meaty jobby!*

But Fergal's alongside him. He's goggling me too, his nose scrunched like it's *me* who pongs.

'When d'you do *that*?' Fergal demands.

Since I'm kinda mildly flattered that he's actually noticed I've *got* hair, I start primping, 'Yesterday. In Carlisle. Pernilla took me for a surprise –'

'You never said in school,' he interrupts.

'I never *knew* in school. What's it to you? You're not

my *boyfriend.*' I'm half-laughing, taken aback by Fergal's grim stare. *You're winding me up,* I'm thinking.

'Puh!' Fergal plants himself in front of me, arms folded. 'D'you *like* it?' His green eyes bore into me.

'What's up with your face?' I giggle at Fergal. 'It's a frizzle. Big deal.'

'But d'you like it?' he presses, and I know I can't bear his stare any more. I might cry. Or tell the truth.

I feel goofy and scratchy. And I wonder what Mum'll –

'Y'know, Foghorn.' My chin must be wobbling or something because Fergal's voice is softer. 'You looked grand before, if you must know. Didn't need anyone changing you . . .' he glances over at Pernilla's car, 'Ach! Girls . . .'

Halleluia! Fergal shuts up. Stomps across the road into the opposite field without another word to me. *Like I've blooming betrayed him.*

'Cheers, Ferg. Totally saved my life with the grub, man,' John calls after him. As Fergal waves without turning, John flicks his hand at the side of my frizzle, his voice hardening. 'Mum'll freak. And why aren't you with her this weekend? I'm DESPERATE to know how her and Dad are and you're the only one who can tell me. But you're mucking about here. Like everything's hunky-dory.'

John's arms are raised, his hands tearing his hair. He's looking at the sky, face screwed so his bruised black eyes bulge out from his brow. His mouth's clamped shut but he's making this high-pitched hum through gritted teeth. Sounds Totally Not Calm, believe me.

'Y'OK?' I squeeze John's bicep. Feel it flex against my grip, not as bulgy as I expected. 'You've lost weight. No drumming here, eh?'

Instead of answering, John hums louder. I check to see if Pernilla's watching. Maybe she can help me out, I'm hoping. Bring John back to Paradise Farm for a couple of days. Feed him up. Lend him some of Phil's old jumpers. Let him soak in my bath . . . But when our eyes meet she toots her horn.

'Big hurry, hon,' she calls out the car window.

'I have to go. You'll be OK.' I shake John's sleeve, knowing fine well he won't be. And I should be staying with him. Helping him.

'Want me to ask Pernilla to telegram Mum about your black eyes?' I bleat.

'NO!' John shouts so fiercely into my face that I half-convince myself his mad-tramp humming routine's a wind-up.

'You just tell Mum I'm fine. OK?' John walks away from me.

You've been hit, I'm thinking.

So what do I do?

Stay to make John admit that Growly Nott's beating him? Starving him? When that'd only make things awkward and complicated.

I'd definitely have to tell Mum.

I'd leave Paradise Farm.

John would end up in ForcesUK.

What good would that do anyone?

I mean, he might end up killed or maimed or toxed . . .

So I get in Pernilla's car. We drive off. And I don't look back and I don't wave and I pretend I can't hear what John's calling after me:

'Molly, *please* ask Mum when we're all going home.'

So there's my **Number 5: MEETING JOHN**. The

unexpected new entry in my Peachy Brilliant Chart. ***MEETING JOHN*** only makes the cut below ***Number 4: SPLISH! SPLASH! GOING SWIMMING*** because it's a tinsy bit less painful than Ouch! Nip! Getting my Ears Pierced (that would be ***Number 6*** if I was having a Top Ten, which I'm not).

As for ***Number 3*** it has to be:

SHOPPING TILL I'M DROPPING ALL SATURDAY AFTERNOON IN CARLISLE WITH PERNILLA . . .

Though to be honest, I've only put it in my ***Top 5*** because it nets me so much pulse gear. The actual *shopping* experience itself is pretty grim. For some reason Carlisle is the only decent-sized town in the UK to have survived The Emergency without a toxing or a bombing and, thanks to a massive flood just after the Millennium, loads of the shops even have their own electricity supply. This means the town centre's flipping *mobbed* at weekends, every shop jostly and over-crowded. Pernilla says half of London come up by train for a day of safe retail therapy.

Anyway, the Best Weekend Ever ends with something soooo peachy it even makes me stop wondering if my 'fuzzy-gorgeous frizzle' as Pernilla calls it, suits me or not. It even stops me worrying about John's black eyes and his bruises. And please don't be thinking that happens because I'm thoughtless.

It's just that *Number 1* in my *Top 5* involves *FALLING IN LOVE*. And love makes my brain go DELETE.

22

Falling in Love

You think I'm joking? Well, *you* don't have the *peachiest* puppy trying to eat *your* toes, do you?

I'm even allowed to *name* this cutie bow-wow Pernilla's arranged for me to meet. 'You like?' she smiles, plopping a towel in my arms then unfolding the corners of it like she's pulling back petals to reveal this fluffball of wriggly gorgeousness.

Do I like?

Even if he squits all over my day-old lemon high-waisters . . .

And despite the farmer selling the pup reckoning he's the *lurvve*-child of naughty Snapper Nott. A temper on him already . . .

And though he bites more than he licks, I *adore* Nipper. He's my all-time **Number 1**!

'I've never held a puppy,' I tell Pernilla, rubbing Nipper's velvety ears across my cheeks. And OK, confession: I'm sniffing back *tears*.

'Never held a . . .? That's *deprivation*,' Pernilla tuts. 'Your Mum's fear of dogs shouldn't mean –'

'Mum can't help being scared,' I butt in quickly before Pernilla says anything more about Mum. She does that sometimes. I don't really like it and on this occasion I must be frowning because Pernilla's voice melts back to the way she usually speaks to me:

'Sorry, sweetheart. Just don't like you missing out on good things. Makes me angry for you. I'm just happy you're happy.' She hugs me hugging Nipper.

'Oh, this is brill. You're brill,' I tell Pernilla when I've finally kissed Nipper for the zillionth time and we're driving back to Paradise Farm. 'Can we go back tomorrow? Puleeeze, Nilly. Gotta see Nipper again.'

All the way I beggy-nag. Even *I* know I'm being annoying. Going on and on about something to Mum never gets me further than a trip to my bedroom to grow up. It doesn't bother Pernilla though.

'So you *gotta gotta gotta* see Nipper again? He's the

best thing *ever*,' she echoes me, giggling till we reach Paradise Farm.

Before we leave the car, Pernilla takes my hands. Suddenly grave.

'I better warn you: Nipper won't always be here. He'll be moving in with a new family once he's better house-trained. That'll be round about your birthday, actually. Which reminds me,' Pernilla's giggly again, 'we'll need to start working on how to celebrate my best girl turning thirteen. Need to do something *verrrry* special. Something you'll never forget.'

'Hey, like what we did last year? It was hilarious,' I start to tell Pernilla. 'You know the song "Molly Malone" –?'

'*In Dublin's Fair City, where the girls are so pretty,*' Pernilla interrupts by singing.

'Yeah,' I cut in because Pernilla's using her high teacher voice and I'm right beside her in the car and the noise is hurting my teeth. 'John rewrote it and him and Mum and my Dad and Adele all sang it to me during my birthday tea:

In Glasgow's fair city,
the girls are quite pretty,
and none are as ugly as Molly, alone.
She's got eyes like a sparrow
and a nose long and narrow.
Down it snotters and bogeys arrive – arrive-o

Then the second verse was totally rude and it went: *'Molly's butt's low and squishy –'*

'Excuse me, Molly, I don't want to hear any more. What an appalling thing for a brother to sing to his sister.' Pernilla takes her hand from the steering wheel and covers my mouth.

'But, no, it was dead funny,' I try to protest. 'Me and John write insulting songs to each other every birthday and Mum bakes a cake and we always take a spong-face photo of everyone and Mum keeps them in an album –'

'As I said we'll need to do something *verrrry* special for your thirteenth.' Pernilla takes her eyes *totally* off the road just to turn and look sorry for me.

23
Missing Mum

Obviously I'm bursting to tell Fergal all about Nipper when I go back to school after my Best Weekend Ever, but when I hurry over to speak to him he scoots into the boys' bogs till the bell rings. While Pernilla's taking the register he sits beside me, arms folded, not whispering insults about the Frizzle Girls to make me laugh as usual. I just think he's mucking about with me so I hold out my knuckle to show off Nipper's cute teethmarks.

'Puppy did that,' I giggle.

'Hope you catch rabies.' Fergal scowls *evilly* at my head. 'Can't believe you didn't go back and see your Mum when you'd the chance. John's gutted.' He snarls so angrily I ask Pernilla to move me to the front of the class to sit with the Frizzle Girls. I thole their gymkhana and tutu chit-chat for four long days but by Friday I'm losing the will to live. Either I shut Sophie Frizzle's geggy by stuffing it with the Pony Club rosette she won't quit bragging about, or I come out with a conversation stopper of my own.

'Guess what?' I shout over Sophie while she's braying about some water jump. 'I've not seen my Mum for nearly a month. Maybe she's dead –'

OK. Extreme – and sick – of me to say what I say but – Halleluia! – it zips Sophie's puss.

Even better, Fergal, who hasn't spoken one word to me since Monday, overhears. He delves into the mewing Frizzle Girl sympathy-huddle I'm stuck in and grabs my sleeve. Wheechs me up the back of the class to my old seat.

'Aw, Foghorn. Mussbe worried sick. Is it getting to you? Not seeing your Mum. Listen. I sort of know how you're feeling. The guilt bit, I mean. See, when *my* Mum asked me to go shopping into Derry with her on Capital Day I wouldn't coz I thought I'd be bored trailing round with her and anyway I just expected she'd be back in no time but she wasn't and

165

I never saw her again and I know if I'd gone with her we'd have gone to different shops than the ones that were bombed and she'd still be alive now and I'm going to have to live with that for the rest of my . . .'

I'm *La La La*, wanting to put my hand to my ears before he's finished. Everything Fergal's blurting out is *so so so* sad.

If I don't blank him, I'll cry for him. Or worse: throw my arms round him while I'm crying. Here he is, still grieving over the worst thing that could happen to anyone our age, and he's thinking about *me*. Thinking I'm missing my Mum. Caring that I'm sad like he must be. He's a good friend, isn't he? And I appreciate his concern, specially when it's translated into slipping me the answers in a French test.

'You don't need any stupid school hassle right now, Foghorn. Y'OK?' Fergal asks. Every. Blooming. Five. Minutes.

Fine, I tell him.

Coz . . . Well the thing is: that's the truth.

And don't be labelling me The Worst Daughter In

The World now. It's just that . . . Well . . . Fergal's got the wrong end of the stick here.

It's not that I *don't* think about Mum. Sometimes. Just that I don't really miss . . . See, compared to Mum, Pernilla does so much more . . . crams every hour with . . . And it's not that I'm not *worried* about Mum, but me and Pernilla do things I'd *never* do with . . . because . . . Mum can't . . .

Oh, this is coming out wrong.

Right: For the record I'm mostly *fine* not having Mum. Pernilla fills the hours with so much peachiness there's no time for homesickness:

One night mermaids are painted on my nails by the same lady who gives me a make-up lesson.

Another night Phil teaches me table-tennis in the garage.

Other nights Pernilla and I go power walking and make toffee apples and our own Sandy-from-*Grease* costumes. We put on a *Stars in Their Eyes Special* for Phil and the Milking Boys. (I'm 'Hopelessly Devoted', and Pernilla's 'You're The One That I Want'. Whoah! Let me tell you, Mum wouldn't get her big toe into one leg of the spandex trousers Pernilla wears.)

Plus I visit Nipper four times in two days. Try to teach him to sit and not to bite. No luck with either!

So. Now can you understand how easy it is to ignore the occasional bubbles of guilt and scaredness that bob up inside me when I catch how Fergal looks at me sometimes; making my temples throb so I can't concentrate on anything but Mum and my Dad and all the bad things that could be happening to them miles and miles and miles away . . . I bet John has moments like this too. When his stomach lurches and his head spins. He prays and prays that The Emergency will leave Mum and my Dad unharmed. He wonders if he'll ever see them again.

The difference between John's moments and mine, though, will be that he has to cope with his scaredness alone on Grumpy Nott's farm. How does he manage to fight it with nothing peachy to divert his mind? Compared to him, I know I'm so lucky. I mean, chances are nothing terrible *is* on the cards for Mum and my Dad.

But deep down, I've a tiny warm glow of comfort

that John doesn't have. It eases my scaredness like a secret asprin:

If the worst comes to the worst, I can stay here with Pernilla. She'll look after me if I never see Mum again . . .

24
An Uninvited Guest

I'm woken far too early one morning by the snorting horn of an army truck which screeches to a stop outside my window. Above the engine noise I hear male voices chanting: 'Moll-y! Moll-y! Moll-y!'

Must be having one of my crazy dreams, I decide, till I open my curtains to a cluster of soldiers round John's age. They're all waving and thumbs-upping me, making *Coo! Look at your big mad hair* shapes with their arms. When their truck trundles from the farmyard in a cloud of gravel-dust there's Mum and her horrible black jaisket standing in the middle of it like she's been conjured up by a ForcesUK magician: *Ta-dah!*

'Hello, darlin'. Couldn't wait another week to see you and John,' she shouts far too loudly at my window.

When she adds 'I've hitchhiked,' a light snaps on in Pernilla's bedroom.

'Hitchhiked?'

Phil sounds *well impressed* when he hurries over from the milk parlour to check out the commotion. Pernilla less so.

'Hitchhiked, Mrs Fogarty? That's a bit excessive. I telegrammed you last week. Told you Molly's wonderful.'

'Well it's been too long since I've seen . . . And I didn't set off hitchhiking . . .' Mum starts to explain to Pernilla but she's already off snapping open pillow-cases and punching cushions plump in the second guest room leaving just me and Phil to hear from Mum how all the rail signals were sabotaged on the Border's line.

'So they put us off the train at Dumfries and I knew I had to start walking if I wanted to get here. That's why I stuck my thumb out for luck.'

'Good thinking,' Phil claps Mum on the shoulder but she shakes her head.

'You'd think so, but I can't have the legs to pick up a lift. After two hours the only motor to stop was that army truck. Driver aimed a gun at my chest and made me keep my hands up while he checked my papers . . .' Mum's flapping her hand to her face at the memory. 'Then he says he's arresting me for Motorway Trespass and Curfew Crime. "Listen, I'm only trying to reach my children," I says. "Haven't seen them for weeks and I can't think straight without knowing they're safe." Here's me blurting away and the next thing the soldier's waving his gun to bring two of his men to help me into the truck. Insists on running me all the way here . . .'

'And more than welcome you are, Kitty. Make yourself at home.' Phil tips his beanie at Mum before he leaves us for the other women in his life.

'So here I am, darlin',' Mum turns to me. 'What's this?' She lifts a clump of my frizzle then drops it. 'Tarty,' she shudders. 'And what's *this*?' She rubs at my mermaid nails with dirty fingers, her mouth down-turned. 'And *this*?' Mum's flicking my earlobe. 'Take the earrings out.' She looks me up and down. Shakes her head. Sighs.

'What?' I sneer, eyes sliding to Pernilla who's

standing in the kitchen doorway.

She's watching us, smiling encouragement at me so I jut my chin at Mum.

'Just because you hate frizzles and make-up and stuff doesn't mean I can't –'

'And with Molly's missing out on so much in Glasgow I felt she deserved *some* tiny treats for a change,' Pernilla's half-laughing as she halts my hands on their way to remove my earrings. 'You *can't* take Molly's sleepers out now. That's plain silly.' Pernilla draws back my hair, tilting her own frizzle admiringly while she shows my ears off to Mum.

'These studs are teeny. Pretty, and all the girls want to wear –' she fusses with my fringe.

'What girls wear should be up to their mothers.' Mum's voice might be quiet but its sharpness makes Pernilla drop her hands to her sides. Then step away from me.

1:Nil to Mum, I'm thinking, as Mum positions herself to stand where Pernilla stood. She cups my face in her hands.

'Your Dad missed seeing you, Molly.' I know

Pernilla doesn't hear this because Mum speaks so gently to me. Yet Mum couldn't have hurt me more if she'd fired the words from a gun.

I sulk over breakfast. Mum's made me feel rotten about not seeing my Dad. So I ask her nothing. Tell her nothing, either.

'So. What d'you do while I was away, darlin'?'

'Stuff.'

'What stuff?'

'Just stuff.'

Well, stuff Mum! Honestly, she's firing all these blooming questions at me. I yawn and slump my head on my arms to shut her up.

Bingo!

'Oh darlin', you're shattered. Me too, after my adventures.' Suddenly Mum's Mum again. Talking my language. Forgiven.

'Maybe we can have a duvet day, darlin'? Catching up.'

Now *that's* what I call a peachy way to spend a schoolday. Unfortunately Pernilla disagrees.

174

'Mrs Fogarty, you disapprove of Molly's *earrings* then you allow her to truant?'

Hand on hip, she tuts at Mum. And I must confess, I'm thrown by her reaction. *One day off with my Mum. Big deal*, I'm thinking.

'Oh, I'm not meaning Molly to truant,' Mum stammers, 'I just think a quiet day together . . . since we've not seen . . . But, listen, if you'd prefer Molly in school then . . .'

'I'll be off in five minutes,' Pernilla tells me as she leaves the kitchen. Silence falls. Mum shrugs and hold out her arms to me.

'Listen darlin', we can't have your teacher thinking I'm a bad mum. She's got a point,' she sighs, leaning in to kiss me. But I dodge her lips. From the yard Pernilla toots the Mini's horn

You're rubbish, my head-voice seethes. *You didn't even act like my Mum there, letting Pernilla boss you about.*

I grab my school bag, slam the kitchen door on Mum and flounce to the car.

'Before you ask, my Mum showed up in the middle of

the night and I'm knackered.' I block Fergal's question with my palm as he bounds over to check. 'She wakes me, moans her face off at my hair and my nails and my earrings, then kicks me out to school so she can go to bed for the day. Ooooh, it's just peachy to see her, I'm telling you!'

Fergal's either gone deaf or stupid on me. Here's me winging and his grin keeps growing wider.

'That's magic, Foghorn!' he beams, pumping his fist in an annoying British tennis-player-style victory clench.

I don't reply. Pernilla's keeping step with me. When Fergal prompts me again: 'Must be grand to see your Mum, eh?' I sense Pernilla asking me the same question: *Grand, is it?* and something about her expression makes me gush, 'Just peachy!'

My eyes meet Pernilla's and I smirk back at her. Though I don't know why. Inside, my heart's jumping up and down with joy at seeing Mum again, yet at the same time something in my head's making me feel ratty about having to answer to her again. I suppose I'm more used to Pernilla looking after me *her* way now . . .

With Mum on the scene, life suddenly feels more complicated.

25
Cabin Fever

But life's not half as complicated as it becomes over the next two weeks as Mum basically ends up moving into Pernilla's second guest room.

Though not by choice.

Mum'd be home to my Dad quicker than she can scoff a Mars bar if it wasn't for the countrywide transport lockdown. The government enforced it after dozens of enemy cells crawled out the woodwork – ironically on the very night Mum appeared at Pernilla's – and randomly landmined train tracks and motorways up and down Britain. Now there are checkpoints and roadblocks and petrol shortages everywhere and Mum's stuck in a place where she's not . . . well not completely welcome, I suppose . . .

Well apart from Phil. He hit it off with Mum from

the moment they first met. Even I could sense this *instant* warmth between them, like they're both ringed with the same Ready Brek halo Mum used to tell me she could spot round me and John if she managed to persuade us to eat it. Suppose me and Fergal were the same when *we* met. Clicked. That just happens with certain people, doesn't it?

On the other hand, sometimes some people rub along *less* well the more time they spend in each other's company: Mum and Pernilla for example. As the days pass on Paradise Farm relations are going downhill fast between them.

Mind you, I can hardly blame Pernilla for being frosty with Mum when they meet for the second time. What with Mum turning up uninvited. Then announcing she's only actually here to take me and John back to Glasgow so I'll be home for my birthday. And *then* she doesn't leave at all.

'Not an ideal situation for *anyone*,' Pernilla tells Mum, same as she tells Mum every time Mum announces, 'I'm going off my rocker stuck here.'

Day in, day out, Mum's complaints are the same:

'I come all this way and I still haven't seen John. Is there no way someone could run me to Nott's place? Please! I'll pay the petrol, any price you like,' Mum begs. More than once she nearly persuades Phil.

'Well, I'm happy to run you to Nott's –' he starts, but Pernilla always overrules.

'But you won't, Phil. And it's nothing to do with money.'

She can *be* a bit on the bossy side sometimes. I've noticed that. Especially with Phil. Or maybe I'm just used to the way Mum and my Dad are with each other. Always talking things out. Hearing what the other has to say.

But day in, day out Pernilla doesn't budge.

'Can't you simply appreciate that your social visit's a non-essential journey for Phil and me? You'll see your son when you're finally leaving.'

'Nilly doesn't want us using up extra fuel with it so short.' Phil's apology is more or less the same day in, day out, except he looks more and more uncomfortable each time he gives it.

All this makes Mum increasingly desperate about John. Some days when I come back from school, she's waiting on the road outside Paradise Farm with her thumb out at Pernilla's Mini.

'Not a sausage been past since this morning,' she reports her failed attempts to hitchhike to Nott's.

'I'm getting cabin fever here,' she tells me on the other days I come in to find her slumped in front of the telly.

'All I do's watch soaps and worry sick about John and your Dad. I'm lounging about here twiddling my thumbs. Pernilla won't have me doing a thing. I'm forever asking if I can bake or tidy or clean . . . "No thanks" she tells me.'

Mum's forbidden to prepare dinner for us. 'That's how I unwind with Molly every day, Mrs Fogarty. Don't you want her to learn to cook?'

And Pernilla's warned Mum not to clean, either.

'Phil and I pay a professional cleaner already. Do you want me to sack her, Mrs Fogarty? When I've a houseful of guests!'

*

Actually, with every day that goes by things between Mum and Pernilla are worsening. Neither speaks to the other unless they have to and – apart from mealtimes – I've started to notice how Pernilla leaves a room whenever Mum walks in. When they do have information to exchange it's done through me:

'We'll be very late home tonight, Molly,' Pernilla might announce to let Mum know.

Likewise Mum's taken to poking her head into the kitchen while I'm helping Pernilla cook dinner. 'I'm not hungry, darlin',' she'll tell me, which translates: *I'll eat the sandwich I made earlier in my room.*

What a stupid way for grown-up people to carry on. Jumblies up my head till I don't know who I should be with any more. If I stay out somewhere with Pernilla that means Mum's alone at Paradise Farm worrying about John and my Dad.

So I worry about *her*.

Feel rotten.

Disloyal.

Can't enjoy myself as much as I could. But if I hang

out with Mum in her room, honestly, she just drones, 'Oh I wish we could go home,' and although Pernilla's not as much fun to be with while Mum's around, I don't want to do that yet. Especially when Pernilla tells me how sad she feels because she knows I won't be here forever and every hour with me's *soooo* precious because she can't have a girl of her own and I make her so happy . . . *That* makes me feel *more* rotten.

Things go from bad to awful the morning Phil stomps into the kitchen from the farmyard and announces, 'Special delivery for Miss Molly Fogarty.' Presents me with a card. Bows.

'Boots!' Pernilla arrows Phil to the doormat. Stands over him while he fumbles his muddy laces undone.

'Glasgow postmark. Secret boyfriend?' Phil winks at me over his shoulder while he lathers up his hands. Ignoring the towel Pernilla's holding out he wipes himself dry on his cow-pooey overalls. Snatches two slices of toast.

'Everyone well?' Phil smiles from me to Pernilla to Mum.

Good question, that.

'*Brrr*. Frosty out there,' he goes on when no one answers.

Frostier in here, I'm tempted to blurt.

Sometimes, I can't be bothered with Mum *or* Pernilla, especially since their pathetic Big Freeze means no one's discussing my birthday.

It's only five days away now! But the pair of them are acting like it's an evil government secret, same as the one about those chemical weapons the last prime minister sold to the countries that are toxing us with them now . . .

Huh! Till this card arrives. No one can deny my birthday *now*.

'Hey, it's my Dad's writing.' I rip into the envelope. Careful, square, my Dad's hand transports me home faster than a trip on a Tardis, and suddenly I'm at his elbow, breathing in the leather and lemony tang of his shaving soap and shower gel . . .

Did you write this to me at the kitchen table, pushing your ginger marmalade to one side, sweeping away any crumbs into your palm before you started? I'm thinking, letting a fifty-euro (peachy!) note flutter to the floor.

Were you in your shirtsleeves, Dad?

Did your pen make little circles of uncertainty above each word before you wrote anything?

Did you use the black one I bought you for Father's Day?

Did you kiss all thirteen xs like you always do on Mum's Valentine?

And does that mean you've forgiven me for not visiting you?

'What's it say, darlin'?'

Mum leans over my shoulder to read the card but Pernilla's dropped the fifty-euro note over my Dad's writing.

'Your Dad's too early. That's bad luck.' She lifts away a plate beneath the card so it closes.

'No, this is *fantastic* luck. I told your dad he was daft posting a card with the mail all haywire, but he said it'd come in time.' Mum answers Pernilla without talking to her. She's standing on the card –'

My card. From *my* Dad. To *me* – in the middle of the table. I still haven't read it. Now Pernilla snatches it up.

'Coo, Molly. A flashing "Groovy Chick" badge. Very pulse for a teenager.'

She's holding the card against her jacket, sucking in her cheeks, preening, scanning me, then Phil for support.

But Phil shakes his head . . . 'Nilly! Behave yourself.' He picks up his boots. Slips out the kitchen before she notices.

Mum shakes her head too, half-smiling.

'Only card your Dad and I could find,' she explains to me. 'Will we read it in your room?'

'Sorry. Didn't know birthday cards were secret in your family, Molly.' Like she's bored, Pernilla wrist-flips the card back at me. 'We stick them on the mantel-piece. Don't we, Phil?' She looks over her shoulder.

Sees she's alone.

'I'll be in the car. Don't be long, Molly.' She bangs the kitchen door on her way out.

'Well!' Mum sighs like she's been holding her breath forever. She pours herself fresh tea, adding five heaped teaspoons of sugar, stirring them noisily. Slurping.

'Let's read now we've peace and quiet, darlin',' she nudges me. 'Your Dad said he'd post this the day after

I left. That makes me faster than the Royal Mail because it's taken over two wee–' From the yard Pernilla's car horn blasts a *Hurry-Up!* warning over Mum's chat.

'Cleaning my teeth,' I tell Mum, hurrying to my bathroom with my card. *Finally* I read:

Your Mum's on her way to bring you back home to Glasgow!
Look forward to seeing my birthday girl this Saturday.
John too!
Fogarty reunion.
With too much love to fit on this daft card!
Your aul' Dad.
XXXXXXXXXXXXX
PS: Kitty, Bring John home too! If Molly's def. just lodging till Christmas, better let the Pearsons know. Safe journey. God bless. D.

'Thanks for telling me.' Forget my teeth. I thrust my card at Mum. 'Home this weekend? Then Christmas?

For good. Does Pernilla know I'm leaving?'

'Who's leaving?'

You'd think Pernilla had the kitchen bugged. She's at the door, car keys jangling.

'Hate to be late, Molly.' She glares at Mum.

'Dad really wants to see you on your birthday, Molly,' Mum beams back.

'You won't be here this weekend, Molly?'

Mum and Pernilla are at it again. Rerouting their conversation through me like I'm the Paradise Farm Wi-Fi box.

'We're definitely going home for your birthday, Molly. Can you make sure your friend Fergal tells John? He's coming too, by hook or by crook. In fact, hang on two secs till I write him a note –'

Mum's planting a random kiss on my head, half way out the kitchen, when Pernilla takes my wrist and whisks me ahead of her.

'No time. We're not waiting any longer, Molly.' Pernilla's ushering me through the front door. Without turning, she raises her voice so it carries up the hall to where Mum is: 'And I'll need to rethink your birthday since you're celebrating *elsewhere*. We might be *very* late home.'

Pernilla probably thinks she's thrown the last punch in this latest round between her and Mum. But not quite. She seems so taken aback when Mum bustles out to the car, waving her arms about and shouting, she actually turns off the engine. No need to, though. For what is only the second time I can *ever* remember, Mum's having a paddy. (The first was when I was out for a walk with my Dad one day at least six years ago. Spotted Mum coming to meet us on the other side of the road. Dashed across to her without checking for traffic. Did I get it in the ear?) This time, Mum's meltdown's got nothing to do with me, though. Well, not directly.

'I might be late back, too, Molly. Since you're too pushed to get a note to your own brother, I'll give him a message in person. Don't you worry yourself, hen,' Mum seethes in at the car window. I can't tell if she's 'hen-ing' me or Pernilla. All I know is she's waggling her finger in front of her face and it's flushed redder than a skelped bot.

'I've hitch-hiked to reach you, I can hitch-hike to

189

him.' *She* has the last word before she storms back into Paradise Farm and slams the door.

'Ooh! Temper, *temper*. Who'd have thought your Mum had such a crazeeee side?'

Pernilla's giggling so hard at Mum's outburst, she can hardly steer the car straight. Doesn't help that she's flooring the accelerator and watching me, not the road.

'I've hitch-hiked to reach you, hen. I can hitch-hike to him. Hen.' In rough, gruff voice, Pernilla repeats Mum's last words. Then goes on, 'That was *scary*. Better keep out your Mum's way till she calms down, eh, Molly?' Pernilla's nudge is my cue to share her mirth. Mock Mum too.

But I can't.

Not when I'm in a panic. Worrying about Mum hitching to see John: *she's not fit, she'll meet dogs, she might get lost*. Worrying more about what'll happen if she actually makes it: *she'll take one look at John and everything'll be over for me here. I wish I could go back and talk Mum out of going to see him . . .*

But I can't do that either; Pernilla's really gunning it, and we're practically at school now. It's too late.

'Hey, Foghorn. Guess whose thumb I nearly ran into this morning on my bike? Clue: you've both got exactly the same smile.'

For a boy who missed lunch writing a punishment essay for Pernilla entitled 'Why I simply can't afford to be two hours' late for school under any circumstances,' Fergal seemed heck of a chuffed with himself. When he finally corrects all the spelling mistakes in his punny to Pernilla's satisfaction and is allowed to leave the baby class and rejoin me in the back row of Upper Juniors, he's full of the joys.

'I made your Mum's day. She told me,' he brags polishing his nails on his school-shirt. 'She said I was her knight in shining armour. She did. Ask her yourself.' He nudges me so many times looking for praise I know my arm's going to be bruised all over if he doesn't . . .

'Quit!' I tell him.

He doesn't.

'D'you know your Mum walked for nearly an hour?'

Nudge. *Aw!*

191

'Not a single car passed.'

Nudge. *Aw!*

'Then me and my bike came down the hill. Stopped for her. Asked if she was OK.'

Nudge. Nudge. *Aw. Awwww!!*

'Aw! I hear you. You met my Mum. You're a knight in shining armour. Big deal.' I pull my arm away from Fergal. His smugness is making me grumpy.

'She's nice your Mum. But she was in some state. Hot 'n' tired 'n' miles to Nott's place. All uphill, I told her that. She'd never have made it.'

'So she hasn't seen John?'

As Fergal shakes his curls at me, relief washes my grumpiness away. *So she hasn't seen John.* Allows me to feel sorry for Mum. *She didn't make it to Grumpy Nott's. She doesn't know what John's going through. And I'm safe,* I'm thinking, returning Fergal's grin at last. Leaning in to him when he beckons me to read something at the back of the jotter he's fishing out his schoolbag.

'I told your Mum to go home then I cycled back up to give John a message. Your Mum said I'd to tell him

192

to come home for your birthday. He wrote this message back. Said you have to pass it on.'

By my side, Fergal whispers John's written words like he's praying them while I read into my head, hearing my brother's voice:

Hey Good Golly Miss Molly,
Reeelly sorry. Luv to b with u but no can do for the birthday bash.
Tell Mum Nott needs me for a pig auction down south somewhere. Oink! OK?
Do NOTT let Mum try to come up here to get me!!! Deffo.
But listen, Mols. Still canny stick this place till Christmas. Nae messin!!!
Save us a slica cake or I'll give you the dumps when I see you.
Kiss Mum. Love you both. And Daddykins!
John.
xxx
Reporting for duty . . .!!!

'Don't get this, Foghorn.' Fergal gives me his biggest nudge of the day before I reach the end of John's note. 'There's roadblocks on the motorway south and Nott's pickup's been out of fuel for weeks. John's going nowhere. You better tell your Mum that. Right?'

Yeah right.

And walk from here to Glasgow via Growly Nott's farm? Think I'm daft. That's what I was thinking while I nodded in to Fergal's green eyes. Thanked him for what he'd done.

'So John was away off somewhere the one day I set off to take him home. Would you credit it? And I thought the roads were tricky and there was no petrol.'

Mum does her spammy-mammy when I pass on the message John wants me to give her.

I can't help gulping. What she says is almost exactly the same as what Fergal muttered while he watched me read John's note.

26
Dream Come True . . .

Must be having another of my crazy dreams, I tell myself when I answer the knock on my bedroom door. The massive box blocking the opening is wrapped in gold paper, tied with red ribbon like a pressie the kids in Disney movies get on Christmas mornings. Giant parcels like this usually only hold one thing . . .

Though that thing never growls like mine does in any of the films *I've* seen. 'Nipper.' I fall to my knees.

Adele. C. Mi Dream Come true!!!
Molly xxx

Except . . . and I know this makes me sound like a six-year-old gonk instead of one day off thirteen, but I've never stopped having a Puppy-Dream-Come-True. In it, though, Mum and my Dad share the moment when

I lift a tiny white fluffball from a shoebox. It licks us all in turn then falls asleep in Mum's hands so she can't help loving it from the start . . .

'Surprise! Surprise!'

It's Pernilla, not Mum or my Dad who shares my Special Moment.

'Big smile, Molly,' she singsongs as a vid-cam glares on. Bling! There's a tripod set in the middle of the hall. Phil behind it.

'Greetings, My Lovely Girl.' Pernilla kneels beside me and proclaims to camera before she bursts into 'Happy Birthday'. 'Your dream come true, Molly. Captured on film,' Pernilla keeps singing as she reaches to pet Nipper. He lunges at her fingers. 'Ooooh, Nipper's as grumpy-wumpy as Molly looks!' Pernilla wags a disappointed finger at us both. 'What's the matter, Molly? Aren't you delighted? Tell you what: let's wrap Nipper back in his box. Film you finding him again so everything looks perfect. Proper birthday girl smile this time.' Pernilla turns up my mouth with her thumbs.

'Sorry, I just can't believe this is happening.'

So blooming early in the morning. It's not even my birthday till tomorrow. And shouldn't Mum be here too? I squint at the camera not daring to guess what my frizzle must be looking like before I tame it with straighteners like I have to do every day now. I try a grin for Pernilla's sake.

'My dream come true,' I tell Pernilla. And I mean it. Sort of. I think.

'One tiny dream. And it's taken thirteen years,' Pernilla whispers. She strokes my face and sighs.

Now I know I'll never be on *Junior Mastermind* unless it takes contestants who add up with their fingers, and I could be wrong, but I've a feeling Pernilla's having a dig at Mum for not letting me have a dog till now. That's not fair.

'Mum's totally peachy letting me have Nipper coz she scared stiff of dogs.' I scoop Nipper into my arms, heading for Mum's room to show off my present.

'You know you're a day early,' I call over my shoulder.

Pernilla grabs my arm. She pulls me back to face the camera.

197

'Well, I'll *miss* your real birthday, Molly,' she clips. 'I was planning a party, till your Mum appeared.'

'Oh,' I shrug, adding, because Pernilla's looking miffed, 'Nipper's better than any party –' I'm still walking backwards towards Mum's room – 'and Fergal's the only pal I'd want to invite from school. John couldn't come. Or my Dad . . .'

Pernilla seems confused. 'But I want *my* friends to meet you, and all my super girls from class would be invited. Anyway we'll still do something. Maybe next weekend? Glam up. New blingy outfits. A real grown-up bash . . .'

Dingy that! Imagine entertaining the Frizzle Girls when I've a puppy to toilet train?

Luckily Nipper saves me the trouble of knocking back the party idea by piddling all down my pyjamas.

'How d'you talk Mum into *this*?' I hold Nipper at arm's length and burst out laughing. Pernilla cuffs Nipper's nose for him instead of answering me. 'Naughty, rude boy!' she scolds. Then turfs him out the door into the yard.

'Nilly?' Phil, who's been quietly filming everything,

abandons his camera. Follows Pernilla outside. 'I thought you *had* asked Kitty about –?'

I'm left in the hall, growing cold, and not just because my pyjamas are soaked. *Mum doesn't know about Nipper yet* it dawns as Pernilla's voice rises outside.

'Shh. Stop asking me your silly questions, Phil. D'you want to wake Mrs F? Spoil Molly's surprise?'

But Phil's doesn't shh. 'You mad, Nilly? That pup's a handful already.'

'But he's Molly's. Not her *mother's*.' Pernilla hurls the words back into the house.

'Molly can't possibly keep a dog if Kitty's not happy –'

'It's not Kitty's happiness we're dealing with Phil!'

When Pernilla slams the door on Phil, Nipper's tail gets nipped as he streaks back inside with Pernilla.

Then all hell breaks loose! Nipper charges down Pernilla's hall trying to sook his sore tail better. Crash! He knocks a hallstand, toppling this massive vase of roses. There's glass everywhere, all mashed up with flower slime and water and a big slick of what puppies do when they're stressed.

'Grab him, Molly!' Pernilla shrieks, but when I reach down Nipper wriggles free. He bolts head first towards the opening at the end of the hall where Mum, in a pair of my Dad's pyjamas, is peering out.

Before Mum can close her door, Nipper's in the room with her. Even *I'm* freaked by the way he growls.

27
A Very Merry Unbirthday . . .

See if that Fergal Lyons yanks my frizzle *once more*, he's getting it!

All day in school he gives it: *Tug. Tug. Tug.*

'Foghorn, gotta tell your Mum John's in a bad way. Don't leave for Glasgow without him.'

Yeah, yeah. Fergal's right. Of *course* I should be reporting how John can't stop coughing.

How he limps on the busted ankle Snapper bit.

How it's infected.

How Mum should know John's run out of tins and toilet paper.

How Fergal's given him a blanket but he's still frozen at night . . .

And I will. Once I'm back at Pernilla's after my birthday. That's only a coupla days: John's hardly going to *die* spending a little longer with Growly Nott, is he?

Is he?

But me:

See if I tell Mum about John *now*, we'll go to Glasgow. And *never* come back. I'd never see my puppy again. That would kill me. It's torture enough not being allowed to take him to Glasgow on the very day I get him as a present. Child cruelty, in fact.

No wonder I'm nipping Mum's head about Nipper soon as we're on that first train home.

'Why couldn't he come? Pleeeeze. I was going to teach him to stop growling and jumping up at you. 'Snot fair! He's my best present *ever*. Better than anything *you've* given me coz you never give me anything I want and just coz *you're* scared of dogs, you want to ruin my *life* –'

'Molly, that's not true . . .' Mum tries to explain herself but it's *la la la* time. I'm on a roll here, splurting out things that are *soooo* nasty, I shock *myself*:

'Bet you don't want me to have Nipper coz

Pernilla's given me the one thing I've wanted forever and you don't like Pernilla and I do, and she knows exactly what I want coz she understands me better than you coz you're old and you don't –'

I'm being so *horrible* you'd expect Mum to nip me back. In the bud. Snap that I should be more worried about bringing John home than any puppy. But she doesn't. Even though I wish she would because the dumb hurtness in her eyes as she takes what I give out to her only makes me behave worse.

Much worse.

On the Edinburgh to Glasgow shuttle I choose a single seat so Mum can't plomp beside me. Leave her to lumber to the other end of the carriage. As soon as she's sitting and her eyebrows are asking me, 'Are you all right there, darlin'?' I open the *How to Look After Your Puppy* manual Pernilla gave me and hold it high so Mum can read the cover. My plan is to keep my arms in this position all the way to Glasgow . . . which would be no problemo if the journey had lasted it's scheduled forty-five minutes.

But guess what? The train's barely out of Edinburgh when it stops. In a tunnel. All the lights go out and stay out. So it's pitch black, and it's cold and the tox-warning siren is screaming whooooeeeewwww whooooeeeewwww like a possessed owl, and in the dark everyone on the train has to fumble on their masks. And after about two minutes of hearing nothing but the siren and having my own sharp panic literally breathed back in to my face, I'm terrified enough to defy the Transport Police warning –

ANYONE WHO LEAVES HIS OR HER SEAT WITHOUT PERMISSION WILL BE SUBJECT TO IMMEDIATE APPREHENSION WITH FORCE IF NECESSARY

– to stumble up the compartment so Mum can gather me against her own thumping chest, lift her mask off and promise me:

'Everything's going to be fine, darlin'.'

And it is. Despite the discovery of *real* explosives in *all* the tunnels we were meant to choo choo through tonight, everything is *fine* . . . As in me and Mum reach our destination in two pieces, not two hundred.

But what's not so fine is that on this my *thirteenth* birthday weekend, I come off the Glasgow to Edinburgh shuttle THIRTEEN hours after I huffed on. I'm a year older. A freezing, starving, grump of a birthday girl. It's five in the morning.

But my Dad's waiting at the station, his smile like a sunbeam on my face.

'My birthday girl. What's all this hair about then?'

I can just about clock Mum rolling her eyes while my Dad clamps his hands round my frizzle to tilt my face up and kiss me.

His beardie scratches and he's so cold that, even after he's let me go to hug Mum till she's practically turning blue from the force of his squeeze, his touch lingers like ice cubes burning my skin. But oh, it's magic to see him.

Though you look older, thinner, I'm thinking . . . or as Mum puts it in front of everyone tripping over the bags she drops to clutch my Dad at the clogged-uppiest part of the barrier, 'Oh Denis, your shilpit face: it's not the size of tuppence!'

205

Mum welds her hand to my Dad's all the way home on the bus. Makes counting out his change a palaver, though he doesn't seem to mind! She's still cleeking him like she's scared he'll escape while he's digging his door key out his pocket.

'Happy Birthday, Molly. Welcome back,' my Dad says as the front door opens and the draught it causes brings down the paper chains he's strung across the hall.

'Hell's teeth,' says my Dad, 'let's just hope the chow I rustled up's not ruined an' all.'

'Oh, Denis,' says Mum, looking my Dad over like he's a gooey choccy-fudge cake. Mum and I follow my Dad through darkness (I check the lights – nothing) into the kitchen where the table's set with the Christmas china. There's white wine open on the dresser, beside it a can of Coke.

'Real Coke, Molly, none of your Saver's pee-in-a-can rubbish!' my Dad boasts. Two red roses droop from Mum's fanciest glasses, their petals shedding on the tablecloth.

'Made cottage pie. Guessed your recipe though

mine tastes nothing like it, Kitty. Swapped half a bottle of whisky for real spuds from Mrs Lloyd downstairs,' my Dad pokes at something in a dish sitting on the camping stove. 'But I left the gas at a peep when I went to meet you. Everything's spoilt.'

'Nothing's spoilt, Denis. Everything's perfect,' my Mum says. Her jaisket's off and she's sitting my Dad down. Pouring wine into his glass. For the first time since we left Nipper I feel all my grumpiness with her dissolving.

'Yeah. Everything's perfect, Dad.'

Well, everything *is* perfect . . . For about thirteen minutes. Long enough for me to gobble my Dad's . . . well it might've been cottage pie once. Now it's pellets of something that reminds me of Adele's cat's litter tray topped with lumpy wallpaper paste. But hey, it's food. Hot. Filling. And my Dad made it.

While I'm scoffing, my Dad hands me a velvet bag tied with ribbon.

'Don't worry, your Mum picked this last time she was here. Not me,' he says, helping me slide this little bracelet over my wrist. It's a bit like one Pernilla bought me in Carlisle, though with smaller pearls and two strands, not ten.

'Now they're real. Not plastic, Molly.'

'Thanks, Mum.'

'And there's more.'

Whoah! A *proper* birthday cake. And by that I mean one that's bought in so it's not humpy-backed like all Mum's sponges. The icing, piped in clone curls, not dribbling down the sides in random squiggles, is topped with a cluster of sugar roses. Circled around the cake are thirteen sparklers. My Dad lights them so they fizzle in the dawn gloom.

'Happy Birthday to you . . .'

Like you'd swear they'd been practising secretly, Mum and my Dad burst into song. 'Cheese!' Mum air-snaps the scene since this birthday she can't find a camera to take a picture. While my Dad puts out the sparklers in his wine I hover a knife over my perfect cake. I'm savouring its beauty almost as much as I'm going to savour its flavour.

My knife barely scores the icing and Mum's tugging me away from the table –

All the sirens –

Tox.

Air-raid.

Bomb alert – begin dro-o-o-o-ning.

Shrieeeeking.

Waaaailing.

Drowning Mum and my Dad's 'Happy Birthday' duet. Instead, the three of us fumble on our tox-masks.

Run!

No time to wrap my cake in foil. Save it for later. No time to grab my Coke.

Hurry!

We're out in the close, down three flights, clattering the metal ramp to our safe bunker.

Move it.

We're jostled against neighbours, everyone pouring underground before the street wardens seal any slow-coaches outside.

Quick!

We're sticking close, Mum gripping my hand, my Dad shepherding us in the span of his arms till we're inside the bunker.

209

None of us speaks. No point. Words can't compete with the corkscrewing siren.

This is real. Not a false alarm.

As if there was any doubt. The crumps I hear might be distant, but they shake the ground enough to shake me. Splinter glass. And the firework-like explosions? I know they're over the hills and faraway, but believe me, I'm happy to be cushioned, safe between Mum and my Dad . . .

Hmmm. Maybe *happy*'s the wrong word.

With nothing better to do my Dad fills most of the hours blathering on about, 'Y'know all this frizzle nonsense spoils your lovely glossy hair. Makes you look the same as every other daft lassie knocking about.'

'Zactly what I think, Dennis,' Mum agrees.

So grateful's better. Grateful we're not gassed like a poor mum and her new baby from the next street who didn't reach a bunker. Or shelled, like Mrs Lloyd downstairs' cousin in Newcastle who was caught – bang – at the epicentre of this, the most vicious attack in the UK yet. Me and Mum and my Dad are alive when the All Clear sounds.

But as for happy . . . ?

Well my birthday's over. Nothing to show for the day but one sad wee bracelet. Can't even scoff my perfect cake when we're allowed home. Or finish my Coke. Everything's binned in case of gas contamination and Posh Patsy's voice warns for the rest of the day: *Stay masked foa six owaz until gas levels reach Safe again . . .*

'Well, there's been a birthday to remember, darlin'.'

Duh!

'It's been rubbish,' I scowl at Mum, which is rotten coz I know fine well *she* can't help The Emergency, but I'm hungry, thirsty, dirty, tired, scared . . .

'Bet I'd've'd a total peachy birthday at Pernilla's. No sirens. More pressies. A party. *And* my puppy to play with . . .'

My Dad's index finger waggles me silent.

'Enough, m'girl. And what puppy's this, Kitty?'

'Oh, Pernilla's present. Awful kind of her but she didn't ask me first. Same as the hairdo.' Mum gestures wearily at my frizzle. She shakes her head sadly at me.

'I know Molly's desperate for a dog. But I can't look

after . . . You know what I'm like with . . .' she begins, then falters.

My Dad buttons Mum's lip with a kiss.

'Kitty, there's no question. Mrs Pearson could've had the courtesy to ask your permission before she gave Molly a pet. If she's not plain daft she's ignorant –'

'She's neither. She's lovely and kind and she feels sorry for me because I'm not allowed anything I –'

'Molly.'

My Dad's look hints I'd be wise to shut my trap and take myself off to my room to cool off.

And that's that.

A very merry unbirthday to *me*.

Bad karma. Bet that's what John would say . . .

28
Highlights of a Braindeath

Yeah. Bad karma. Because I'll give you the other highlights of my birthday weekend now:

See! No other highlights whatsoever!

'*Me no jest,*' as John would also say. If he was here. But he's not. And I miss him. Even to fight with. And I worry about him too. Lots . . .

It doesn't get a whole lot better *after* my birthday either:

I'm stuck in Glasgow.

It's November dreich.

There's no hot water.

No fresh food.

Most of the shops Mum trails me round have empty shelves.

Yup, it's all pretty much a braindeath. Well, OK, not entirely *all*. Not my trip to Tangles hairdresser's. Though I don't exactly jump for joy when Mum tells me I'm booked in for a restyle. Her personal birthday present.

You see, even though I know within two seconds of being snipped that my new urchin-style suits me miles better than my brillopad frizzle I feel I have to kick up at Mum, "Snot fair, you made me lose my frizzle. You're always telling me what to do. Pernilla never does that.'

'Poor Pernilla,' Mum clicks her tongue and nudges me as we leave the salon. 'Now you don't look like a clone of her any more . . .'

'What d'you mean "poor" Pernilla? That's rich. There's nothing poor about her,' I turn on Mum but she just smiles into my scowl.

'And I must admit, these look so pretty now.' Mum touches the tiny sleeper studs in my ears, which is her saying sorry for making such a stramash about two winking dots of gold. 'And you're getting so . . .' she sighs.

Pulse, I'm thinking. *Grown-up. Glad Mum's made me do this*.

'The double of your mother when she was a punk. Not as wild. *Nearly* as beautiful!' my Dad ruffles my urchin when he sees me. This, by the way, is during the two-minute window when he actually quits his precious paperwork to talk to the girl who was forced home to spend quality time with him even though he's hardly ever *been* at blooming home . . .

Most of the time I'm stuck in our flat with Mum who's just so happeeee doing her housework and cooking and running after my Dad I wanna screeeeeam the house down:

LET ME OUTA HERE!! Because Adele's still gone –

Where r u?? Mss u 22222 much.

– but worse than that, me and Mum are trapped in Glasgow, unable to get back to Pernilla's.

That's right. My birthday weekend stretches to *fourteen nights* in the end. On the Tuesday morning we were *supposed* to leave for Pernilla's, every railway station in the UK goes on Top Level alert and closes. Next morning the motorway south is strafed from end to end during rush hour. All I'm going to say about that is that the radio coverage I catch before Mum turns off makes me grateful our telly's kaput.

'Right, Molly. What activity's going to keep our minds off John today?' Mum asks each morning once her tranny's confirmed there are *still* no citylinks and sentences us to another fridge-less, bath-less, Pernilla-less day in Glasgow.

'Bowling? Bingo?'

To be fair to Mum, as soon as she's done her daily

216

Mrs Mop 'n' Shop she makes a point of getting out and about in Glasgow.

'Bombs or no bombs I want us to do something interesting every day you're here,' she's decided. 'This is a great city, and we should make the most of the bits of it still standing.'

Guess what? I actually have to confess that in between my huffs and hissy fits and *When can I go back to Paradise Farm*? winge-sessions, *loads* of the things Mum and I do together are pretttty peachy. Daft. Fun. Mad.

Like us heading to the Botanic Gardens one bucketing day. Rain was so bad the park was empty so we did a 'Singing in the Rain' routine with our brollies along a row of benches, me and Mum puddle-stomping and shouting and laughing at the top of our voices. Fergal would have loved it, though I bet Pernilla would have been mortified if she'd seen me acting so outrageously.

I know she'd have *died* if she saw how Mum and I carried on one day – a day when there was Actually Power: Yahoo!!! – and we wandered through the Art

Galleries and started comparing the size of Mum's bum to all the nudies in the painting halls. She'd pose next to a big fat Rubens or a Rodin sculpture and stick out her boobs and her bum and pout till my knees were so weak from laughing I could hardly stand . . . Best hoot I've had for ages.

And another afternoon when there was *power again* – yahoo! – we hurried to the Grosvenor Cinema. Guffawed all the way through a rubbish action movie with wrinkly old Tom Cruise acting like he was still young and unwrinkly enough to be the hero. Which – even though Pernilla think's he's sexy – he's *so* not.

'Never was, ferrety-looking twerp of a fella,' Mum says. Still, you can't knock two hours in front of the big screen eating popcorn . . .

In the fortnight we're stuck in Glasgow one of the other things that happens is that I grow used to Mum being My Mum again. Slow and fat and grey and unfashionable. *Soooo* different from Pernilla. But not in a bad way.

Mum's just Mum. And she's so comfortable and so content, just being home, with my Dad.

'This is the life, Denis,' she cuddles up to my Dad every night. ''F it wasn't for fetching John, I'd just post off our lodging's cheque. Never go back to that farm.' It's weird, actually. After two weeks, I'm practically Calm being back in Glasgow myself. I thought I'd miss Pernilla and Phil more that I do. Maybe there's just nothing to beat being around to see my Dad off to work in the morning. That has to be one of the peachiest things about home.

'Missing you already,' I'm there to tell him.

29
The Letter Bomb

This big slice of my heart wishes I could still be home to kid my Dad, 'Missing you already.'

But as soon as the railways were running again, me and Mum were on a train.

So now I'm back at Paradise Farm. And it's funny, I miss my Dad more than ever. Though not as much as I miss Mum.

Sounds spammy, saying that. Since she's back here with me, isn't she?

But she's not *here* here.

My Paradise Farm Mum is sad. Slow. Glum. Like all her lights switched off as soon as she stepped from the Border's train. Face tripping her. Opposite of the mum I had for two weeks while we were back in Glasgow. *That* mum was full of life and music and daft jokes. She was cheery and giggly and daft. She kept bursting into song for no reason and doing crazy spur-of-the-moment things like dragging me and my Dad along to a belly-dancing class one night and . . .

Posting a cheque to Pernilla even though she knew we had to return to Paradise Farm.

It's in a letter I snatch – *just* in time – from Nipper's gnashers. Someone has to catch the mail the *instant* postie shoves it through the letterbox these days. Otherwise Nipper totals *everything*. No wonder Pernilla prefers to keep him in the barn.

While I'm on the subject, I'll confess that my Dream Come True is a nightmare. Nipper's *so* not cute any more.

He's a snapping, crapping handful and in the fortnight we've been apart everything about him's supersized: height, weight, teeth, temper, turds, bark . . . The Discipline chapter in my puppy manual doesn't *begin* to cover the kind he needs i.e. Canine Boot Camp. No way could he live up our close in Glasgow, and you know what? Secretly, I'm glad.

Anyway, the mail I've rescued –

'Looks like your writing, Mum,' I say, handing Pernilla a slimy envelope.

'Glasgow postmark. I've no friends there,' Pernilla slides her eyes towards Mum as she slits the letter open. She's *still* not spoken to her. Not since she clocked my urchin over a week now, turning pale and wide-eyed-blinky as she took my hands.

'Molly, did you catch something nasty back home? Ringworm? Lice?'

'Miaow!' Mum had chortled at that one. She's not chortling now though. No, she's heading for her room.

'Ohhh. Thought that letter'd already come. Thought that's why she was giving me the bum's rush since we came back. She won't like this.' Mum's hands are flapping at her chest.

'She won't like what?'

'My decision. But it's made.' Mum actually sounds firm. She's speaking from the other side of her bed-room door.

'What decision, Mum?' I call over Nipper's growls.

Silence.

*

Though not from Pernilla.

'Frankly, Molly, I'm unbelievably hurt.'

We're driving to school and Pernilla's still sniffly. She spent so much time locked in the toilet with Mum's letter I thought we were going to be late. Now I'm worried we'll be late as in *dead*. She's driving to school like a complete bampot. Talking like one too:

'After all the treats you've . . . After I mentioned I've booked *skiing* for New Year? Could she *ever* give you opportunities like . . . ? And then Christmas. All the cards I've ordered with you part of . . . Oh why's she taking you away *now* when we're so . . . ?'

'Are y'OK, Nilly? You're all shaky.' I offer Pernilla a biscuit from my lunchbox. 'Mum goes crabbit and wobbly when she skips breakfast like you did today –'

'Why would I be crabbit and wobbly like your Mum, Molly?' Pernilla interrupts me. 'I'm *nothing* like her, am I? And how can I *possibly* eat?'

Still driving, she delves into her handbag for Mum's letter. It's all scrunched up. She shoves it into my hands. Handbrake parks. Hurries into school without waiting for me.

I'm left with the piece of paper that's changed everything:

Dear Mrs Pearson,

Thought I should let you know Molly and I are stuck in Glasgow till the railways are running. I am sending you a cheque for this month's lodging anyway plus notice that Molly will return to Glasgow as soon as I make contact with John. Evacuating my children has not worked out as I imagined. I didn't know John would be lodged so far away from Molly. Not having heard from him in weeks, I am worried about his welfare. Despite the risks of The Emergency, and the prospect of compulsory evacuation if war continues, I believe it's in the best interest of our family to stick together until then.

We appreciate all you have done. Molly has loved lodging with you and has been very happy. You and Phil have been so good to her. She will miss you both and I am grateful for the welcome you have shown her.

Yours truly,
Kathleen Fogarty (Mrs).
PS I am sorry but we will not be able to keep
Nipper.

Gulp. I can't believe Mum's given Pernilla notice without telling me. It's all feels very sudden. And final.

As I watch Pernilla disappear into school I can't help having this sensation of the ground between us shearing away and a big yawning hole opening up.

30

All I Want for Christmas

I try to tell Fergal what's going on before class begins.

'Guess wh–'

'Total and utter silence,' Pernilla interrupts, her eyes narrowing on Fergal. 'I'm not in the mood for nonsense.'

Before retiring behind her corrections, Pernilla adds that anyone caught chattering will be sentenced to a week of maths lunchtimes.

'Write four pages in your story jotter: "All I Want For Christmas". Lots of detail and no baby mice in your stocking please, Mark Jones.'

'Finished,' Fergal nudges me. I've barely scribbled 'All' let alone worked out how big I'll need to make my writing if I'm to cover *four* whole pages.

'You're at it, Lyons.' I snatch his jotter.

'See. Not writing any more. Who cares about Christmas stuff?' he hisses while I'm flicking his pages to count.

His essay's only four giant words long. Each letter gouged into the page of his jotter:

MUM MUM MUM MUM

'None of her business what I want,' Fergal whispers when I slide his jotter back. In Total and Utter Silence.

See, this surgy feeling is making me want to touch Fergal's arm. Blurt, 'Hey. Sorry.' How spammy would that be? So I change the subject. Slip Fergal Mum's letter.

'I'm leaving soon.'

'No, Foghorn!'

Get this. Fergal actually seems . . . Well who knows what boys are really thinking? 'Gonna miss me?' I simper. Can't help myself.

Fergal recovers too flipping quickly for my liking.

He crosses his eyes, licks his lips slabby and – yeeuck – *puckers* up.

'Want my Christmas kiss early, Foghorn.'

'Wouldn't blow you one through my butt,' I whisper, topping off with a raspberry that splurts Fergal out laughing. Then I wish I hadn't because he noogies my head. I've to chomp down on my tongue so I don't squeal while he's reading Mum's letter.

''Bout time too,' is Fergal's verdict when he's done. 'Sucks you're going, but John can't stay with Nott. By the way, I've not seen him for days. What d'your Mum say about his leg and those bruises and . . . ? Oh, oh, trouble ahoy, Foghorn . . .'

'Why in the world are you reading my private letter, Fergal Lyons? Give and get out, please!'

Before I have to confess to poor Fergal I've *still* reported nothing he's told me about John to Mum, he's being banished to the baby class.

Even though I'm the one who's written zilch.

'I'm so disappointed, Molly,' is all I get after she's shredded Mum's letter. Flung the scraps in the air. When Pernilla's sitting back at her desk I feel her eyes on me. There's a flat smile on her face but I can't tell what she's thinking behind it. Just sense she's Not Calm. That's why I knuckle down to my stupid essay. I'd rather eat Nipper's turds than do extra maths.

'So, Molly. You really got stuck into your work once you'd peace from that *pest* Fergal. That's my girl!'

Driving away from school Pernilla seems bags cheerier than she was in class.

'I can't wait to read your Christmas wish list,' she giggles. 'So tell me what you want, what you really, really want?' she urges. 'That's the only reason I made the class do this. Bet you want loads to wear. Maybe frizzle extensions till your lovely hair grows? Or what about the opposite? Leg hair lasering? Phil bought me that two years ago.'

'Er, I didn't really write about wanting any *stuff* coz y'know how Christmas is meant to be . . . sort of more than shopping and spending, and anyway I won't be here –'

'Puh! *"Christmas is more than shopping and spending"*,' Pernilla parrots me sourly.

'I can guess who told you that. Listen. You ask me for *anything*. That's giving *me* a gift, actually because all I want to do is make you happy.'

'I can't think right now,' I tell Pernilla, though I don't add it's because I'm thinking of Fergal. One thing he wished for. One thing money can't buy. One thing Santa can't deliver:

MUM MUM MUM MUM.

I shrug. 'Honest, I've everything I need, Nilly –'

'Oh, for goodness' sake,' Pernilla bangs the steering wheel. 'Forget *need*. What d'you *want*, Molly?'

I shake my head. Look out the car window wishing Pernilla wouldn't snake the country roads so fast. As her headlamps tunnel orange cylinders through the duskfall, they throw images from my mind into the darkness like twin projectors in a moving cinema. I'm watching the Christmas wish list I ended up writing for Pernilla come to life even though I tried really *really* hard to think up the sort of *stuff* she would approve of.

But suddenly I just couldn't push beyond this ache to see the skyline view that used to clutter my bedroom window-frame two floors up in Laurel Street. Before The Emergency, that is. Back then I could see the graceful spire of Glasgow University piercing the sky. The glass peaks of the new BBC Scotland headquarters. The red brick spread of my Dad's shipyard. His office.

That was before the university spire was bombed from the air and the BBC building was flattened when a man swigging from a bottle of Irn Bru, that wasn't really Irn Bru, walked into reception and detonated himself. My Dad used to point out all these landmarks, holding me while I knelt on my window ledge, mapping the places I recognised with a smudge on the glass. The memory of being with my Dad's still so vivid I can feel, not the edge of Pernilla's car seat, but the press of wood against my legs. My Dad's hands gripping warm on my waist, the cold gold of his wedding ring before it warms up on my skin. I even smell bacon from the kitchen. Hear Mum interrupt whatever song she's been singing: 'John. Dennis. Molly. Breakfast.'

The sigh my memory's made me breathe out has clouded Pernilla's car window with sudden homesickness. It's thick enough for me to scrawl a

231

decent insult throught it with my finger. Like how I used to write *Pie, Loser, Gonk* every time I *huhh*-ed on John's gleaming cymbals.

Now I'm seeing John in the headlamp cinema. He's thrashing away behind his drumkit, peroxide hair flopping all over his face. Grinning. Eyes closed. Totally lost in the beat, man. Adele and I used to creep into his room while he was pounding. We'd stifle giggles, dance all wiggly in front of him. Oh, Adele . . .

Ohhhh Adele . . .

She was so brilliant, specially doing that shimmy dance where you hold your nose and pretend to sink underwater. Like someone famous off the telly she was. Her and me'd mimic John for so long without him sensing us we'd forget we'd come into annoy him in the first place. End up caught in the music, dancing for the sake of dancing, till John clocked us. Then he'd chuck his sticks in the air.

'You're history, my little ones!' he'd roar. Grab us. Tickle us to tears.

Now different tears than those hysterical ones blur the memory of John: him crushing me with his great big beefy drummery biceps. Adele's giggle-shriek.

'Penny for you thoughts?' Pernilla pats my knee.

For Christmas I wish me and my family and pals could go back to the way things were before The Emergency then I wouldn't feel so mixed-up about going home. Because everything in my head's so jumbly. Half of me wants to stay with you and Phil, Pernilla. To be special and spoiled. But another part of me wants my family together. Muddling along and ordinary. It's like my heart's being tugged in two directions at once . . .

'Don't have any thoughts,' I lie.

31
Everything Blows Up

Pernilla flicks the car radio back on. Instead of music, a woman speaks in a Very Bad News voice:

'. . . *Impossible to estimate the extent of the devastation* . . .'

Pernilla beeps the next channel:

'. . . *Cannot confirm the death toll* . . .'

She changes waveband. This time the broadcast's live. The newsreader's voice broken-up and jagged:

'. . . *Endured massive casualties on a scale unseen in Scotland for decades. On both sides of the river* . . .'

'Give us music, not misery.' Pernilla jabs for a new channel.

'. . . *Seems the Clyde shipyards were the specific target –*' a different reporter says. He sounds spookily like Keith, John's dead mate.

Is it the memory of what happened to *him* – blown

to so many bits by a train-bomb that his mum and dad had nothing to bury – or the news I'm jigsawing together that washes a cold chill over me? Makes me lean towards the radio.

Bombardment . . .

Clyde . . .

Glasgow . . .

Carnage . . .

Shipyard . . .

SHIPYARD . . . Where's my Dad? . . . *my* Dad . . . Dad . . . DAD . . .

Words are repeating. Sinking in as Pernilla swings the car into Paradise Farm.

'Hey look, Molly: Phil, my husband. He's actually out of his milking parlour in daytime! Honey, I'm home,' she trills.

Shoosh, I nearly snap.

'*Fierce fires are hampering attempts to reach the –*' Keith-not-Keith says on the radio until Pernilla blasts her horn at Phil.

'Ooooh, why the long face on my handsome hubby?' Pernilla pouts at me.

I don't laugh.

I've sussed why Phil's looking upset. Why he pulls off his beanie as he opens my door. *'Someone's a goner, Molly . . .'* Mum always used to say when police-actors do that on telly.

'Molly.' Phil speaks gently. Then sharper, squinting his eyes like he's worried how Pernilla's going to take him sounding forceful for a change when he says, 'Nilly. The shipyard where Molly's dad's been . . .' He squeezes my arm. 'Now listen to me. Your Mum's had no definite news but the milk boys have taken her in my van to fetch John. She's wanting everyone home.'

'Yes,' I gulp, 'I know.' *I must. In fact I should be there already. Not here. If I'd told Mum about John sooner I'd be there now. Maybe my Dad's work wouldn't be hit if I was in Glasgow. Maybe everything would be different . . .*

'What? Molly's going back to Glasgow.'

Pernilla reaches from the car and grabs my wrist. 'Please. Not yet –'

'Nilly. Get a grip. Not now.' Phil breaks Pernilla's hold on me. Opens her door. Signals her to climb out.

'I'm away to check trains. The main roads are closed else I'd be driving you,' he tells me, starting the engine. When he tries to pull away in the car Pernilla grabs his window sill.

'How can we let Molly leave? And what kind of mother would take a child back to a war zone? I've been there. It's dreadful. Molly should stay here. Make her stay.'

'Nilly,' Phil silences Pernilla with a frown. He's pointing to his van. Tom's at the wheel. He's speeding towards us across the farmyard.

'Oh, Molly. Is going what you want? Really? Think of yourself. Your future.' Pernilla turns to me, her arms outstretched but I don't know how to reply.

I've just been hit with a bombshell. My legs are that shoogly and my stomach's that churny I bet I'm going to puke.

Then Phil's van door opens and I see Mum. She's edging out the van backwards, trying to find a foothold so she doesn't fall and her horrible black jaisket's ridden so far up her body as she stretches from the cabin that the milk boys and Phil and Pernilla get a right good eyeful of her plobbly ab-less tum.

'Remember,' Pernilla murmurs, her fingers digging my shoulder, 'if you don't want to leave I'll look after you for as long as –'

'Oh, Molly.' Mum practically severs Pernilla's arm from my shoulders to tug me against her. Her whole body's shaking, 'The worry of your Dad's bad enough. Now John's missing too.'

All Mum's weight's round my neck, making my legs buckle. She's choking me so I sound evil. 'John's missing? When? How?'

'You tell me. Your friend Fergal said he told you he hadn't seen John for days. You never said to me, Molly. Or that he was black and blue. Now he's disappeared. He's only a teenager –' Mum's hands clutch her chest. Her voice rises in appeal to Pernilla. Unusually for Mum there's an edge to it.

'And John's a good boy. Why couldn't he have just lived here with Molly when there was work for him? She's been in clover while he's sleeping rough in a barn. Half-starved. Knocked about. Did you know that?' Mum jabs a finger at Pernilla.

Then at me. 'Did you, Molly? If you did, you never told me –'

'Mrs Fogarty! You're terribly, terribly upset.' Pernilla pushes Mum's finger away from me. Tries to steer her towards the farmhouse.

But Mum lashes her away.

'Upset? Just because I'm needing home to my husband but I can't leave without my son. Upset? I'm demented. If you lost a son you'd be demented too.'

32

The Last Straw and Supper

On this, my last ever night at Paradise Farm, things are as Calm as they're going to get. The milk boys are still driving round the countryside putting out feelers for John, though nobody seems to have seen him. Phil, shovelling down a snack in front of the telly, promises he'll be straight back out to join them.

While he's refuelling he insists on Mum having a break from the rolling news, especially since it reported that the stealth plane flown into my Dad's work hit the canteen during his lunch hour.

So things look . . . I don't even want to say. But just in case there's a miracle and my Dad stumbles out of the chaos in Glasgow, I've given Phil the photo John snapped at his last-ever school sport's day of my Dad looking like there's a flagpole piercing his skull.

'Girn like you're in agony,' John directed so it's not a good likeness. Just the only photo Mum has left.

My Dream Come True pulped the rest.

'Oh dear,' Pernilla tutted, when we saw what Nipper had done to Mum's belongings while the farmhouse was empty. 'I don't think you can have shut your room properly, Mrs F.'

Mum gasped. Bobbly jumpers, comfy old shoes and Fogarty family photographs were strewn the length of Pernilla's hall.

Chewed up. Spat out. Mashed.

When I went for the big pants hanging out of Nipper's mouth, he went for me – teeth sinking my lip.

'I hate him,' I couldn't stop myself bawling. This was The Last Straw with my Dream Come True.

As Pernilla hauled Nipper off me, she roughed his back.

'I'm only a silly *pup*,' she wuffed in a kid-on doggy voice. 'Just playing. No one's any fun round here.'

That's when Mum grabbed Nipper's collar. Bundled him out of Pernilla's kitchen.

'Enough,' Mum muttered, kneeling to gather her possessions. I helped. There was next to nothing worth saving from the little she'd brought. Maybe a plastic bagful.

'Oh Mum, your clothes.'

'Don't fash, Molly,' Mum told me. 'What do clothes matter? Anyway, no point being laden if we're on and off trains. You need to travel light yourself.'

'Definitely travel light.'

Phil keeps echoing Mum's advice to me while he reads the travel bulletins scrolling along the telly screen.

'Trains'll be haywire tomorrow. Something to eat and drink's the main thing.'

'Well, if luggage *is* rationed, I'm helping Molly pack all her lovely new clothes,' Pernilla insists, her voice all choky as she ushers me away from Mum and the telly to my room. Emptying my drawers and wardrobe she pyramids the contents on to my bed.

Whoah! There's *so* much gear I don't know what to pack, where to start. Pernilla's matching all the socks she's bought me. She's lining them up on my dressing table.

'I wish you could stay with me. You *could* stay with me,' she whispers while I lunge for a single pair of socks.

'I'll take these. That.' I snatch a T-shirt before it's folded. 'Don't like Mum watching the news on her own,' I tell Pernilla. But she isn't listening. She's fanned out all my tops and is running the back of her hand along them like you'd stroke a kitten.

Shaking her head. Eyes closed.

Since I don't know what to say to her, I tiptoe from the bedroom.

33

Weird and Getting Weirder

Well past my bedtime now, me and Mum are still huddled in front of the telly. Even though the shipyard bombing in Glasgow's old news now. The new news is that someone's popped the prime minister's bodyguard.

I'm feeling weird, my head buzzy like when I've a temperature and my stomach's all churned like I've overdosed on milkshakes. I feel worse than the times my Dad used to wake me in the middle of the night singing, 'We're all going on a summer holiday'.

At least when my Dad bundled me into the car, then vroomed the motorway for five hours while me and John tussled on the back seat, I knew there was a fortnight of sandcastles and melty 99s to make up for the queasy journey. Tonight, who knows what's waiting at the other end of these slowed-down hours?

A dead Dad?

A disappeared brother?

Our family blown apart by this stupid, stupid Emergency . . .

You should see poor Mum: she's picking her fingers bloody. Clutching her stomach. 'John, where could you be?' she moans. A lot.

La la la I kid myself on I don't hear her, even though I'm worried sick about John myself. When Pernilla suddenly glides up to Mum and puts an arm round her I feel I'm blacking out.

'Kitty, someone's brought news about John.'

'News?'

The Smurfy-blueness of Mum's face is weirder than Pernilla calling her Kitty. When Mum tries to stand, her legs won't support her.

It's police with their hats off time, Mum must be thinking as she collapses on top of Pernilla, pinning her to the settee.

'Eek-eek,' Pernilla squeaks.

'Everyone all right?' A man calls too cheerily to be a hatless cop. Weirdly, he looks like Fergal Lyons on stilts, wearing a grey curly wig. I know he's not Fergal though. That's because Fergal himself is helping this curly man heave Mum upright.

'Would you look at you legless ladies, and not a drink among you! Guy Lyons.' The man unlocks Mum's hands from my fingers and clasps them in his.

'Kitty,' Mum stared blankly up at him.

'I married a Kitty, didn't I?' Guy Lyons darts a smile at Fergal. 'But to get down to the business in hand, I believe there's been folk round looking for your lad while I was out on business. Well, I'm here to report he's off to Glasgow on my old boneshaker.' Guy Lyons smiles and pats Mum's hand. From the settee Pernilla puhs a blast of disapproval.

'John took your bike . . . ?' Mum winces.

'Borrowed,' Fergal and Guy Lyons chime in unison.

'Where's the note, Da?' Fergal says.

'Oh, I can't read anything,' Mum says, smoothing the scrap of paper Guy Lyons fishes from his pocket. 'Molly's dog chewed my specs.'

'Let me, Mrs Kitty,' Fergal leans over Mum's shoulder. 'Dear Mr Lyons,' he reads John's words in an Irish accent.

'I've been labouring for Mr Nott but now I'm going home to see my Dad about something. Ferg said you never use your bike so I hope you don't mind if I borrow it. If I don't return it I swear to pay you back out my first wage. That'll be soon. Promise.

John Fogarty.

PS Ferg didn't OK this, though he's baled me plenty.

So, hey, Foghorn,' Fergal lands me a shoulder punch. Ouch! 'John'll beat you home.'

'Home?' Mum's goes spammy-mammy as she fingers the note.

'Your lad'll be well home, Kitty,' Guy Lyons takes Mum's flapping hand in his. 'And if I'd only known the trouble he was in with that gom Nott –' he flashes a look at Pernilla – 'there'd've been something done sooner.'

'John knew Molly was happy here and he didn't

247

want to worry you either so he put up with . . .' Fergal gives Mum a sheepish shrug. 'But he left about five days ago. Just had enough –'

'And I didn't know?' Mum blinks at me so I have to look away.

'Please God all's well. You've troubles to seek already.' Guy Lyons grips Mum's shoulders before he turns to leave.

'Well, I just hope you're repaid for your bike, Mr Lyons,' Pernilla sniffs as she opens the sitting-room door. 'That young man should have asked you before he –'

Guy Lyons shakes his head till Pernilla's words peter out.

'Get this straight, Kitty. Your lad owes me *nothing*,' he reassures Mum. Then he rumples my short hair.

'You'll be the Molly Foghorn I'm never done hearing about. "Molly says this" and "Molly does that". His lordship tells me you're –'

'Da,' Fergal hisses darkly. He slinks from Pernilla's sitting room.

'Bye,' he mutters randomly.

That's him leaving. I might never see him again. Another pal lost . . . I realise, and I don't know, maybe my feelings show on my face because Mum nudges me.

'Quick. Better give Fergal our address –'

'Grand idea. Once things settle I'll bring his lordship to Glasgow next time there's a chess-set auction to see his –' Guy Lyons sweeps his hand vaguely around me.

His what? I'm wondering as Mum shooes me to find some paper and a pen.

In the dark of Pernilla's hall, Fergal's slumped against a wall studying his thumbnail like it's *really* interesting.

I throw a casual, 'Your dad wants my address,' over my shoulder as I pass him.

'So I'll give you my mobile and home phone and Hotmail for when stuff's working again. Means if your Dad decides to visit at the last minute . . .'

'NO NEED TO SHOUT, FOGHORN,' Fergal shouts. Right in my ear because he's right at my elbow. Must have followed me into Pernilla's study. When I jump up from the drawer I'm opening, and he sees how startled

I am by the nearness of him, he grins. Then rumples my hair like his dad did.

'Sorry.'

We're face to face.

'What are you giving me then, Foghorn?' Fergal asks in his normal voice. And for a mini-micro-teeny-tiny second we both hold each other's gaze, and – I'm not joking I stare into the greenness of his eyes and . . . *oooh* – *something* (Don't ask me what, just something) fires up and sizzles – *whoosh!* – like flame between us. We both jerk away from each other like we've been burned.

'Paper . . .' I fumble in the drawer, fumble for words, doing my stupid best not to blush.

Suddenly Fergal reaches his arm alongside me.

He's going to . . . This is my first . . .

Adele. HELP!!!! Mollyxx

No. And I'm not going to say what I

Think.

Hope.

Wish.

Fergal Lyons might do next.

Because he's a gonk and he blooming well DOESN'T.

He just brays, 'Hey, Foghorn. Check you with your stupid fuzzball!'

Fergal's arm was only touching mine because he's delving for a photo in the drawer. It's stuck to a card pinned to the lid of a box. Fergal lifts this out.

'Ha Ha!' he hoots, jabbing his finger into my face. Not my *actual* face but the one in the photograph he's found.

OMG. How unpeachy was I with that frizzle?

That's the first thing that shocks me when I snatch the photo from Fergal. It's that self-timer Pernilla made Phil set up the morning last month when my Dream Came True. Phil's standing behind me but my hair's so big you can only see the top half of his face so I can't tell if he's beaming at me as adoringly as Pernilla in the photo. Her arm's round my waist, pulling me close to her. Don't think I've ever seen her more content.

Unlike Nipper. *What you looking at suckahhh?* the photo could be captioned.

If it wasn't already captioned.

Because it's a Christmas card. One of those cheesy personalised embarrassments us Fogartys – even Mum – always crack up over. Especially if the card includes a smug *Aren't-we-all-brilliant-and-don't-we-have-such-crazzzzzeeee-fun-in-our-soopa-doopa-family?* round-robin letters inside. Last year John fought me till my nose was bleeding to win first-graffiti rights to one of *these* cards. What the heck would he say now if he saw me staring out at him from the front of *this* card? Especially since what's it says is more shocking than my frizzle:

SEASON'S GREETINGS FROM ...
THE PEARSON FAMILY AT LAST!!

'There's stacks of these. Look.' Fergal picks the top card from inside the box. Opens it.

'"*Happy Christmas love Phil and Nil and Molly and Nipper.*" Thought you were going home, not moving in for good with *her*.' Fergal tuts. 'Huh. *Now* I know why you never told your Mum anything about John. You didn't want to mess up any of *this*.'

Fergal skites a hand off the card in disgust, shaking

252

his head so hard that a draught from his curls flicks my cheek. A shiver runs down my spine, warm and cold all at once.

'Ferg, I dunno anything about this. I *am* leaving. Tomorrow. Swear,' I whisper, urgent for his approval and very puzzled.

'Well, what the hell's this? It's freaky.'

Together, we hold the card between us, our arms touching properly. We don't move apart. Don't realise Pernilla's behind us till she speaks.

'Molly, I've been trying to find the right time to talk about this.'

34

Unbelievable!

'Better write, Foghorn.'

We're all at Pernilla's front door. Fergal jabs my upper arm.

I dunt his chin.

'You'll be lucky.'

'Look after your Mum. She's the only one you've got,' Guy Lyons interrupts. While he's busy squeezing Mum in a gangly hug, Fergal grabs my hand with both of his. 'Hope your Dad and John are . . . Seriously, Molly, wish you weren't . . . y'know . . . You have to . . . but I wish you could . . .' he whispers. Squeezes. Keeps holding till his dad ushers him out.

'Now, while you're here . . .'

Fergal's silhouette hasn't cleared the glass of Pernilla's

front door, but she's already steering Mum away.

'It's an awful time to bring up something to do with Molly,' Pernilla says.

'What's she done now? Is there more about John she was meant to tell me?' Mum's voice slumps as heavily as her body when she sits down. Her eyes shift to the telly.

'Nothing. She's an angel,' Pernilla trills over the king droning his daily message. 'Will I switch off, Kitty?'

Without waiting for an answer, Pernilla angles her seat to block Mum's view of the screen. Beeps the remote.

'Now, Kitty,' Pernilla does one of her teacher claps to make Mum focus.

'Phil and I want to make you an offer,' she smiles. 'Well *I* want to make you an offer. Don't I?' Pernilla beams over Mum's shoulder just as Phil slips in the back door. Then her smile drops.

Because Phil's nursing a bloody hand and his mouth's open to explain his injury.

'Boots!' Pernilla growls at him in Squishbutt's voice.

'News yet, Kitty?' Phil ignores her. He squeezes Mum's shoulder.

Mum shakes her head.

'Your hand?' she asks.

'Nipper got me bigtime when I dropped him back where we bought him. Good riddance there, Molly.'

'Oh, don't worry. Your next pup'll be good-natured. I'll guarantee it. Fancy a Lab?'

'Pernilla's voice is sweet again.'

'Not if we're leaving,' Mum answers flatly. Before she finishes speaking Pernilla takes a deep breath.

'Well, that's what I . . . and Phil . . .' Pernilla exhales.

'Not now, Nilly. Not after today . . . You shouldn't . . .' Phil rubs the stubble on his chin, shuffling his socks on the carpet. Looking *really* uncomfortable. Especially when Pernilla nips back quicker than my Dream Come True.

'You want me to wait a week, darling? Ask then? When it's too late?'

Before Phil answers, Pernilla turns to Mum.

'We know *you* have to go home, Kitty,' Pernilla begins, 'but can't you let us keep Molly? Like *adopt* her. For good. There. I've said it now . . .

Me and Phil . . .

Think. No. I *know* . . .

And so do you, I think . . .

Molly's life would be much . . .

Well, let's face it, than you can . . .

So why don't I become her . . .

Oh, and I know it's a terrible time with your poor husband . . .

But Molly'll leave here and . . .

Oh, Kitty, she's so happy . . .

Ooooh. I can give her every . . .

Look. No disrespect, Kitty . . .

You're *wonderful* for someone your . . .

But we're *young* . . .

And you're . . .

We just want Molly so much . . .

You still have a son, after all . . .

When Molly leaves, I'll have nothing . . .

And I'll be such a good . . .

Oh, let me keep her . . .

I promise, no one'll ask questions . . .

Lots of people disappear into thin air during this Emergency . . .

So we'll just say *you're* missing in Glasgow . . .

Presumed dead . . .

You say Molly's missing too . . .

Then just leave her to me to adopt . . .

And go . . .'

I watch a pulse throb in the jut of Pernilla's collarbone. She digs her knuckles into her knees and stares into Mum's face.

Mum's chest is rising and falling, her breathing harsh and irregular because she's shaking her head and squinting at Pernilla's mouth like she's expecting more mad, mixy-up words to spill out. There doesn't seem to be any fresh air going spare because I don't feel as if I'm drawing in anything when I try to fill my own lungs. Pernilla wants to *keep* me. Be my new mum.

What if Mum says yes?

What if Mum says no?

What would my Dad have to say if Mum arrived home without me?

What's happened to m'girl?

Molly Pearson, the inside-my-head voice tries on the new name for size without me knowing it's going to do that. Guilty, I swallow the sound away. Don't want Mum thinking I'm practising being a new me.

She'd think I want Pernilla to be my new mum.

I don't.

Do I?

Do I?

I don't know what to think. That name: *Molly Pearson* is clanging round in my skull. Echoey. When I close my eyes to make the voice stop, all I can see is a Christmas card Mum doesn't know about: Me and Phil and Nil and Nipper – The Pearson Family At Last.

'But I've already got a family.' I think my head-voice is talking to itself. But no. I've spoken aloud.

I open my eyes when Phil squeezes my shoulder.

'Of course you have. There's your answer, Nilly.' I think he murmurs before he leaves the room, though his voice is so low I can't swear if he spoke in words or if his brain just e-mailed mine.

Mum and Pernilla remain, both smiling at me like I'm the first chocolate doughnut in Gregg's the baker's window for eighteen months. But they're not smiling the same smile. Pernilla's turns her mouth and eyes and even her nose crinkly. She looks like she's been holding in a surprise and now it's out she's bursting to know my reaction. And Mum's smile isn't even really a smile. It's too sad and her cheeks are clapped in. When her eyes search my face their expression tells me that it's hurting her to look at me because she loves me so much. I just *know* that without her needing to speak. And her barely-there smile swallows me until . . .

Well, this sounds spammy but without Mum touching me I feel her arms round me like when she spoons me to sleep after a bad dream.

'Oh, it's a great business,' Mum's sighs through her bruised smile. 'Imagine anyone but me and your Dad prepared to put up with your smelly feet and your singing, darlin'?'

She's shuffling from the sitting room when Pernilla bounds after her.

'Mrs Fogarty. Kitty? I know this is such a bad night to ask, but your answer . . .?' Pernilla's voice is shrill and desperate. 'Can I keep Molly?'

Mum's reply is soft.

'Now, that would have to be Molly's choice.'

35

It's Make Your Mind Up Time

Eeeny-Meeny Miny mum

Both are kind and both are fun.

Both mums love me soooo

Which one?

Which?

Mum?

Do?

I?

Choose?

Tough decision?

'Oh, Molly. *Please, please, please* let me keep you.' Pernilla dives at me before Mum's even out of earshot.

Her perfume swirls round me like sweet nerve gas. 'I'll make you so happy,' Pernilla promises. 'We'll shop and swim and travel and you can have a dog or a cat or a guinea pig or a cheetah . . . You can have anything you want.'

'Peachy.'

I'm nodding in time to Pernilla's temptations. I'm thirteen. Someone's offering me the moon on a plate. 'So it's a yes? You'll stay? Oh, sweetheart! I just *knew* you'd choose me. Honestly, you're doing the right thing.'

Pernilla's gripping my upper arms in her long fingers. Nails digging me. *Ouch!*

I think the pain kick-starts the sensible part of my brain.

'See if I lived with you, would Fergal be allowed round?'

From the look on Pernilla's face you'd think my request was one of John's satanic farts.

'Fergal? *That* Fergal? Oh, I suppose . . . though when you're boarding there won't be time to . . .'

Excuse me?

'Boarding?'

As in Malory Towers? Hogwarts? Chalet School? Posh girls with trunks and tuck and lacrosse sticks?

'Well, the school I've chosen's pretty far away . . .'

'I move here then you send me away?' I double-check.

Pernilla flaps the air between us like it pongs.

'Molly, I couldn't send my *daughter* to a *village* school –'

Daughter. What I'd be to Pernilla if she keeps me sounds cold. Formal.

I'm just Mum's girl, her lamb, her lassie, her darlin' . . .

I shake myself free of Pernilla's hold. In my mind's eye I'm seeing –

Mum. *Always* waiting to meet me at the end of every single school day:

The maths-test days.

The sore-tummy days.

The yay!!! Squishbutt's absent, hope she's dead days.

Even Mum's bad lankle days . . .

Split second I appear in the schoolyard Mum separates from whoever she's gassing with to ask:

'How was school, darlin'?'

No matter the weather. No matter the mood I'm in, *Missed you, Molly,* Mum tells me. *Lovely to see you.*

If I stay at Paradise Farm I'll miss Mum telling me she misses me . . .

'Mum says boarding schools are cruel.'

'Expert, is she?' Pernilla rolls her eyes to the ceiling.

'If I live here, can Mum still visit me?'

'Oh, I really don't think . . .' Pernilla stuttery-sighs. *'I'd* be your mum. You might feel confused if you saw her.'

'And what if I'm here for a while then decide I want back to my real mum . . .'

'No. You choose between us. End of story.' Pernilla looks straight ahead of her. That's my final question to her.

But the first I ask Mum.

She's whorled on the futon. Which she's cracked. Hasn't told Pernilla yet.

'Another oopsident – me tossing and turning over John and your Dad,' she explains when I coorie into her. Her tranny hisses between her ear and the pillow, and the sleeve of her shiny black jaisket lifts my hair with static as her fingertip tickle-traces my earlobe.

'I've a feeling your Dad's waiting for us. You know when you're sure about something inside? Can't get home soon enough to see him. Can you?' she whispers, like she's checking I've cleaned my teeth, assuming I have. She seems more interested in fiddling with the reception on her tranny than hearing my answer.

So I shrug.

'See if I live with Pernilla for a while. Check it out. Then want back to you . . .'

Mum kisses my neck. Her arms tighten round me with her shrug.

'Fine by me. You know you're my girl forever. No matter where you are, who you're with. End of story. Same as John's my son no matter what.' Mum switches from talking to humming along to this country song I've heard her and my Dad sing together.

'Better tell Pernilla tonight,' Mum murmurs as the song fades.

'Tell her what?'

I'm nearly conked out.

'You're coming home.'

'Am I? How d'you know I'm not going to . . . ?'

Mum shoogles herself tighter against me, nylony sleeves shooshing out whatever I'm sleep-slurring.

'As I say, you always know when you're sure about something inside,' she murmurs, punching me gently where my heart is.

I'm too sleepy to ask if she's talking about me or herself.

36

Fisticuff Fairwell

Now it's my last morning. Phil's knocking on Mum's door.

'Wakey wakey, Kitty. An hour till your train.'

His words remind me of my Dad. A lifetime ago. Him waking me and John to come *tothefarmtothefarm- tothefarm*. I know I'll miss Phil. Lots.

'Oi, rise and shine before I deal you a wet facecloth,' Phil's calling me now, banging my princess door at the far end of the hall, thinking I slept there. So quickly I'm up, unshlooping my face from Mum's arm, hoping I can scuttle along to my bedroom before Pernilla clocks me wearing yesterday's slept-in clothes. I'm more crumpled than a fish supper wrapper the morning after the night before, my hair poking up clumpily and my face scarred from lying on the seam of Mum's jaisket sleeve all night.

I can't say goodbye to Pernilla looking like I've spent a long night in some safe bunker. The next couple of hours are going to be tough enough without her giving out about the criminal irresponsibility of a parent letting a child go to bed without cleaning her teeth or washing her face. I don't want to deal with *any* extra hassle than the one I'm bound to cause when I come out with these words I've memorised: *Pernilla, I want Mum to be my mum.*

I'm dreading a showdown as it is.

I'm really sorry. It's been peachy living here with you and Phil but I'm going home. That's what I'm rehearsing in my head while I'm pulling down the handle of my bedroom door. My mouth feels dry so the words I've prepared earlier collect into a massive ball in my throat and stick there. I'm gulping it away when I hear Pernilla. Inside. Talking to Phil. Waiting for me.

'You're wrong, Phil. Molly's made up her mind to stay. The sooner you dump that fat old frump lump at the station and get her back to Glasgow, the sooner Molly's life really begins,' Pernilla's hissing.

I hurl myself into that room like a hand-bomb.

'Shut up!' I silence Pernilla, scary as Adele when she loses it with Julie B. Then, before I can stop myself, I blare, 'I'd *never* live with someone who slags off my Mum behind her back. *You're* horrible. Don't wanna stay here anyway –'

'Oh Molly. Shh. I'm not horrible, and you must –' Pernilla gasps. Tries to catch my wrist, but I fling my arm high, away from her.

'Sweetheart.' She reaches for me again. 'Listen, I'm just being honest. Cruel to be kind. You're Mum's such a sloven. Can't you see? Overweight, unfit and old . . .'

'Shut up. She's not. She's –'

'. . . unfashionable, out-of-touch . . .'

'Nilly, that's enough . . .' Phil puts himself between me and Pernilla, holding up the flat of his palms to silence her. But she ignores him. Her voice grows shriller with every word she says.

'If a woman like that can't even look after herself, she doesn't deserve one child let alone two. And definitely not a girl like you –'

'Stop saying these things. Shut up. You're *evil*.' I'm screaming into Pernilla's face when Mum shuffles into my bedroom in her baffies and horrible black jaisket and my Dad's pyjamas.

'What's going on? Something the matter?'

'Oh, would you look at yourself!' Pernilla actually stamps her foot when she rounds on Mum. 'You'd choose *that* over me?'

When Pernilla flaps her hand in Mum's direction, she scowls and her face turns all twisty and ugly like a layer of her beauty has peeled back to reveal something lizardy underneath. I can't believe someone who's been so lovely to me can be so mean.

'God knows what Molly sees in you. Or your husband, that's all I can say,' Pernilla sneers. 'He must be *desperate* –'

'Nilly. For God's sake. Mind your lip.' I've never heard Phil's voice so sharp as he finally silences Pernilla. By now I think even *she* knows she's crossed a line because she stuffs her hands in her mouth and starts wailing like a wounded animal. Scary *and* sad that is – I mean, what if I *had* chosen to stay with Pernilla and she suddenly took the hump with *me* like she's done with Mum? Yes, scary and sad, though not

271

as scary and sad as the wash of pain that the mention of my Dad brings to Mum's face. She actually staggers so Phil and I have to lunge and grab her.

'Nilly.' Phil glares his wife from the room.

'I'm sorry, Kitty,' Phil puts his arm round Mum's shoulder. 'She's so desperate for a girl and Molly's been the best thing . . .'

'Listen. You've nothing to be sorry for. Go after her, darlin',' Mum takes Phil's hand and holds it to her cheek. 'Tell her it's all right. Know what it's like to love a child.'

Mum's free hand punches her heart with her fist. She's smiling. Slowly. Sadly. Kindly.

'Just time me and Molly went home.'

37
Fogarty Reunion

'Look, hunners of wee boys,' Mum calculates. Aloud. While we force ourselves into a train compartment already jam-packed with soldiers all spic in their sludgy green ForcesUK uniforms. 'New recruits, God love them.'

Mum points out the spammy amber-feathered eye-squishing bunnets the soldiers are wearing. They're crammed so densely that once I'm on the train, I can't see to a window to check if Phil waited to wave us off.

Maybe he's already speeding back to comfort Pernilla.

You'll have a girl yet, Nilly. Promise. We'll keep trying.

Or maybe he's just heading straight to the milking parlour and a normal, straightforward, long, long, placid working day of Tom and Jack and pop quiz competitions on the radio. And the comfort of his nuzzling, lowing brown-eyed girls who never answer back, never boss him about . . .

D'you see Phil? I turn to ask Mum. Then don't bother. What's the point?

That final hour at Paradise Farm is a blur already. Dreamlike.

Pernilla, standing in the farmhouse doorway, was ice-cold when we parted. Her face completely blank while she watched me and Mum dumping our bags in Phil's van. You'd swear we were complete strangers to her.

Can't believe you wanted to be my mum I was thinking when I walked over to her. Whispered, 'Nilly, thanks. For everything,' rising up on tiptoes to peck her cheek. Nearly losing my balance when she stepped back from my kiss.

'I'll write,' I told Pernilla. Though I knew: *Will I wheech*. Pernilla gave no sign she'd heard my empty promise. Just waited till Mum hurried towards her, 'Look, Pernilla. You've been so –' Then slammed the front door on us both.

'End of story,' Mum sighs as the train pulls away.

Not quite.

Though for a good chunk of the ride nothing eventful happens. Mum doesn't come over all faint or announce she feels sick. She doesn't hyperventilate or spammy-mammy. She just stands beside me, head bowed.

'Talking to Denis. Letting him know we're on our way,' she tells me, eyes closed tight. So I don't disturb her, even though I'm wondering if her head's nearly bursting full of my Dad, like mine is.

If she can hear his voice:

How's my best girl?

Feel his rough kiss on her cheek like I can.

I even smell the shampoo he uses: Boots Family. Maybe one of the soldiers has just washed his hair in it.

And I see my Dad too. And not just the one of him. There are – ooh – easily as many Dads thronging my head as there are soldiers in our compartment.

One Dad's still buttering those lunch pieces he made for me and John the day we left Glasgow.

Another Dad hurries along our landing. Head down. Raincoat flapping. Remembering to stop and wave back despite his rush. Blow Mum a kiss.

A different Dad cleeks me and Mum through the park on a Sunday afternoon when the leaves swirl our ankles and the rain slashes our faces. He's chortling that the three of us are like the reverse of his favourite painting in the Art Gallery. This saucy lassie in her bonnet and best dress strutting arm in arm in the sunshine with two guys . . .

'. . . Looks right smug with her lot, eh, Molly? Picture's called "Two strings to her Bow". D'you know what that means?'

Yet another Dad nudges me, reading the label off the actual painting he's been talking about. Hand on my shoulder.

Course I do. I've had two strings to my bow: Mum and Pernilla. More complicated than you'd think, I feel myself mouth an answer.

Ga-ga this must seem? Here's me, wedged between Mum and a gangly soldier who's chewing Juicy Fruit with his cakehole gaping and my head's thronged with Ooompa-Loompa-sized Dads. And I'm talking to them! How insane is that? And if I say some of my Dads are in better health than others, not all of them walking and talking and conscious, can I leave it at that?

Change the subject, please?

Move on to what happens when Mum rummages this cash 'n' carry-sized packet of Werther's Originals from her handbag and passes it around our carriage.

'Just feeding your boys,' she tells, rather than asks, this polished-up officer who bears down on his recruits when he hears sweetie papers rustling. Mum looks him up and down like he's a giant Werther's Original himself.

'Oooh, you're like a film star in your *sexy* cap. A young Ewan McGregor, isn't he, Molly?' Mum nudges me.

Pure cringe, Adele. Beam me up!!

I'm dying off at Mum's cheek, even though the officer laughs away the compliment with a salute.

Mum salutes back. 'I've a son the same age as these fellas. Put him to farm labouring to keep him out of uniform. Isn't John ages with these lads, Molly?' Mum nudges me, though from the gasp I give you'd think she'd stabbed me in the ribs.

No, John's probably younger, I decide, making a quick

search of the faces. Suddenly, seeing all these soldiers I'm in a panic: unlike Mum I *can* see John buttoned into a uniform. In fact I'm half-expecting him to jostle his way through these recruits: *Hey, Mum. Hey, Mols. I'm Action Man.*

Didn't John threaten to sign up?

As my eyes dart round the compartment so many things about these soldiers remind me of John I could howl. Some have dimples like John's when they grin, others the same raw-red blotchiness of the shaving rash John hates. Some drum their blunt fingers to private head-tunes the way John always does when he's uptight, while others do what he does when he's edgy: chew at the skin inside their bottom lip . . .

'Listen.' I've a horrible feeling I need to warn Mum. 'See, when we get home, don't go crazy if John's joined . . .'

I'm tugging Mum's sleeve, trying to get her attention, but she's too busy gabbing with her officer to heed me.

'Where you fellas heading anyway?' she's asking. 'Or is that classified? All the way to Glasgow would cheer me up,' she nods and smiles at her new friend, but his smile inverts to a grimace.

'We *are* going to Glasgow,' he shakes his head slowly, 'though I'm afraid it's to recover bodies from the rubble of yesterday's shipyard . . .'

'You're joking.' Mum's not smiling any more either. 'That's where my husband . . .'

The officer just catches Mum in time. Once he's thumbed two of his men off their seats so Mum and I can have them, he coaxes her to give his soldiers a full description of my Dad.

'You mustn't give up. We need a name. Age. Anything we can use to identify your husband, Mrs –?'

'Kitty. Not Mrs Kitty. Mrs Fogarty. That's my husband. He's not Kitty. He's Denis, and awful ordinary . . .'

The attention of these soldiers on top of the shock of *why* they're on our train has Mum wasted.

'I'm all discombobulated,' she spammy-mammies as dozens of young guys huddle round her, passing the description of my Dad to those who can't catch what Mum's saying first hand.

'Mr Fogarty is average height.'

'And he'll be wearing his glasses.'

'Mr Fogarty wears spectacles.'

'With a gammy leg. Keeps falling off.'

'Attention. Mr Fogarty has an artificial limb,' the officer bellows. 'Would that be the left or right leg, madam?' he asks Mum.

'I can't mind. Keep telling him he needs a new pair but he just sticks the leg back with Sellotape –'

'Strike the artificial leg, soldiers,' the officer interrupts Mum. He's beginning to sound like he's sorry he asked for this description.

'And my Denis is a bit thin on top. Grey. Like his eyes. No, they're not thin.' Mum smiles so warmly at a point in front of her that I look there too, expecting to see . . . Well, I can guess who she's seeing.

'Just grey. Soft grey,' Mum whispers to herself.

'Grey eyes. Grey hair,' barks the officer. *That'll do*, his brisk nod means but Mum's on a roll now.

'And he's a lovely smile. Hasn't he, Molly? Dimply. Funny how you and John smile the same . . .'

'Show them your photo, Mum' I snap before Mum

makes me do one of John and my Dad's smiles for a carriageful of guys. That would not be Calm. As that gonk snap of my Dad with the flagpole poking out his head is passed around I watch each soldier's face. And d'you know what? Not one recruit so much as sniggers. Every guy handles the photo carefully by the edges. Some of them have trembly fingers.

'Promise we'll keep our eyes peeled, missus,' the last soldier to see the picture nods at Mum.

'God love these boys,' she whispers, putting the photo away. 'They should be out on the tear, partying and seeing bands like me and your Dad at their age. Like our John's going to be doing when he starts Yooni. Teenage boys shouldn't be on journeys to God knows what's waiting . . .'

38

Reporting for Duty

What's actually waiting when our train trundles into Queen Street Station is a Massive Police Presence. Armed. Walkie-talkied. A crackly announcement over the tannoy warns all civilians to stay on the train. **REPEAT: STAY ON THE TRAIN.**

We're being Indentichecked before we're allowed off.

So, from our seats, me and Mum watch the recruits gather their kitbags. Not one of them passes Mum without some remark or other before they're mustered on the platform.

'Ta for the sweets.'

'We'll be keeping an eye out for that squinty leg, missus.'

'Keep your hopes up.'

'Just do your best,' Mum murmurs. She's still footering for our Identicards as a transport policeman approaches. This means she's not watching our soldier-friends tramp past the window like I am: leftrightleft-right. Not wondering, like I am, why they fall out of rank into chaos well before they reach the end of the platform.

Scattering. Shouting. Some running back up the platform as far as our compartment. 'Something's happening,' I gasp, seeing a soldier with hair as black as Fergal's overtake the others running with him. When he reaches our window he thumps it with both fists, gesturing me and Mum off, jabbing his head down the platform.

'Out of order there, soldier-boy.' The transport cop on the train unholsters his gun. Hair-like-Fergal's been joined by the Juicy-Fruit chewer. They're drumming the window so hard the glass ripples.

'Quick,' they're bawling.

'Stay where you are, ladies,' the policeman warns us.

This means Mum and I witness what happens next through the train window. It's bigger than the plasma screen Adele and her mum had to leave behind when they went to Canada and its size kind of suits what's unfolding because, honestly, it's more like the movies than real life anyway. All the soldiers are clustered outside our train window now. They're whooping and cheering like they're all extras in one of those cheesy war films where no one important ever gets wounded or killed and everyone throws their hats up in the air at the end: *Huzzah!*

In the middle of them stands the Ewan McGregor officer. He's giving me and Mum his salute again though we can only see his head and elbow and cap. This bewildered-looking grey-haired man in squinty-legged held-together with Sellotape specs is blocking our view of the officer's shiny buttons . . .

See what I mean about the whole scene being like something out a film?

Course. Since it stars us Fogartys it's more like *You've Been Framed: The Movie* than a slick blockbuster.

Yet again we give ourselves an *epic* showing-up in Queen Street Station. This time it's my Dad's fault. The transport policeman with the gun decides he's guilty of Threatening Behaviour because, when my Dad spots me and Mum through the window, he barges like he thinks he's a superhero on to the train without showing his Identicard. Mum doesn't even get kissing him before he's horizontally manhandled back up the platform by six burly transport cops. On the station concourse – teeming as usual, they slam my Dad to the floor. Draw their guns.

'Don't move. You. Are. Under. Arrest.'

And yes! This stramash draws quite a crowd, which doubles as soon as Mum starts thwacking the policemen off my Dad with one of her shoppers. From the clonk it makes against the policeman's head, I think she's using the bag that holds her tranny. And from the way it drips yellow slime over his uniform I think I've tasted the last of Phil's lovely free-range eggs . . .

'That poor man was bombed yesterday,' Mum wails so wretchedly that all the soldiers from the train surge towards her and the Ewan McGregor officer pulls very loud rank on the transport cops.

'Release this civilian. He survived yesterday's

atrocity at the shipyards and now you're delaying my soldiers attending the rescue there.'

My poor Dad. He might not be going to the poky but he's so stunned by the rough handling that he stays flat out on the station floor after the transport police have melted into the crowds and the soldiers have leftrightlefted from the station.

'Legless again, Denis,' Mum says, bending over to help my Dad up. She's pointing at the specs dangling off his face.

Of course, she has to lose her balance, doesn't she? Ends up spreadeagled across my Dad, splatting him.

'Welcome home,' he grunts. 'And, my lovely girl.' He waves up at me. Not smiling, I notice. *Something's wrong*, my stomach clenches, and the spasm it sends through me turns my joy at seeing my Dad alive and in one piece to something crabbit and sour.

'We thought you were *dead*. Saw the shipyards on telly. Kept looking out for you . . .' I'm snapping at my Dad while he pushes Mum off him gently. Tries to sit up. His cheeks look grey and sad. Inside I'm feeling a right cow, but that doesn't stop my narking, 'I mean

286

when we heard about the bombing we thought . . .
And we were miles away. You could have sent a
telegram . . .'

My Dad shakes his head to silence me, pulling an
orange paper from his raincoat pocket.

'I'd have sent a telegram to say I was fine if I hadn't
had this one already,' he says, smoothing the creases on
the typed page for us to read.

'I'm only alive because I couldn't stomach work
yesterday. First day off I can remember taking in years,'
he tells Mum while I'm reading:

```
TO JOHN/DENIS FOGARTY. STOP.
MOLLY/KITTY HOME MORNING CARLISLE
TRAIN. STOP. PLEASE GOD ALL SAFE.
        STOP.F/G LYONS. STOP.
```

'Look, Mum. From Fergal and his dad. That was
pure decent –' I hold the telegram out, but Mum
doesn't take it.

'Denis, you sick or something? You're awful pale.
Awful worried looking –' Mum's trying to pull my Dad

round to face her but he keeps turning to peer round the station. Searching for someone, I realise, sensing his distraction. Mum does too.

'John?' Her hands go to her chest. 'Please don't say he never came home.'

'Oh, Kitty. Kitty. He came home.' My Dad has tears in his eyes though his voice is fierce, and his knuckles are white as he balls the telegram from Fergal and shakes it in his fist. 'And he'll tell you he's better than all right when you see him. And he's that proud of himself . . .'

'So he's here? Where?' Mum's smiling. Breathless. Relieved. Flailing between me and my Dad to see if she can spot John.

'Kitty. Wait.' My Dad interrupts my Mum's excitement. He heaves her to her feet.

Draws her arm through his. Walks her towards the station exit.

'I'd be dead if it wasn't for what John's done.'

'What's John done?' Mum's voice is quavering.

'Saved my life yesterday sacrificing his to this . . . He's a bl–' My Dad never swears, but I'd say he's close when he whips round. He's frowning into my eyes.

'Why didn't you tell me John might do this, Molly? If I knew I'd have found him other work so he'd be safe . . . He says he mentioned joining up to you but your head was turned with shops and swimming pools and hairdos and . . . and anyway –' My Dad turns back to Mum. He sighs and draws her close against him. 'John says there's no choice for his generation . . . only a matter of time . . . it's he's duty to serve . . .'

'Denis, what are you taking about, darlin'. What's the matter?'

I don't need to wait for my Dad to answer Mum. I'm already running through the station, through crowds of commuters and soldiers and security staff. Behind me, my Dad's voice rings so clearly it's like he's miked to a secret earpiece I'm wearing.

'. . . John's leaving tomorrow . . . to be trained to kill . . . expects he'll be sent to the desert . . . All the time Molly was telling us he was fine on that farm John was planning . . . Kitty, prepare yourself . . .'

'John!' I call, dodging in and out of masses of recruits like the ones on our train.

'John. John. John.' *Sorry. Sorry. So sorry. Should've told Mum everything. Should've listened to Fergal. Should've been less selfish.* In my head, I'm crying till one of the recruits steps in front of me. He holds out his arms wide so I run into them.

'Hey, Mols. Check me out! Action Man.' John crooks his knees so we're eyeball to eyeball. Beneath his amber-feathered bunnet both of his sockets are still bruised plums. There's a gash on his lip too. When he grins at me it starts to bleed.

Ouch! I wince for John, but he's not bothered.

'Private Fogarty, reporting for duty.' John doffs his cap and spins round to show himself off. Spins round like I used to when I dressed up in yet another new outfit from Pernilla. Like this is fun. Like this is a joke . . .

'Hey, Mols, why the long face?' John tickles me with his amber feather.

Instead of giggling, the stroke of it makes me cry.

'You're a soldier and it's all my fault . . .' I'm wailing but John takes my shoulders and shakes me gently.

'Yeah, this is your fault, you dafty.' John sounds

delighted. 'You didn't want me to quit Nott's coz you were scared I'd be killed if I joined up. Ferg didn't believe me but I *knew* that's why you never told Mum how tough that bloody farm . . . that bloody Nott . . .' John stops grinning at me and shaking his head like he's proud. He closes his eyes, puffs air through his cheeks. Lets his hands drop to his sides. His shoulders slump. He seems miles away. In a bad place.

Then he recovers. 'Anyway, Mols,' he shrugs, 'I'd no choice but to leave. I know everything was magic for you, but that psycho Nott was gonna kill me. ForcesUK's gonna be paradise compared to all that. Beds 'n' regular grub 'n' pay 'n' I'm in a marching band already so I might be their drummer boy, leading out the troops. In't that *wild*. Girls're just gonna be fallin' at my feet – Hey. Whassmatter? I'm sorry . . .'

John grips my shoulders. Pulls me against the rough serge of his uniform.

He's sorry, I'm thinking. Sorry for *what*?

'Mols, don't cry. Please. The draft was only a matter of time. Don't really have any choice. It's happening to everyone my age. Better to join up as a volunteer – you get treated better . . . That's what I told Dad. And if I can survive Nott's, I'll survive The Emergency. It's Calm.' John's gripping me tighter, trying to make me meet his eyes again.

'Please keep it together,' he urges me.

And his voice is scared and desperate and low.

'For Mum. Don't let me down for Mum, Mols,' he begs.

I won't. This time I won't. I look into my big brother's eyes and promise just before the force of Mum's hug slams John against the station wall, and me and John and Mum and my Dad are all together again for the first time in months.